EPIC,
The Electronic Publishing
IndustryCoalition

Presents

New Voices
2011

An Anthology of
Winning Entries from
The New Voices
Young Writers Competition

The Electronic Publishing Industry Coalition

Welcome the Voices of the Future

EPIC, the Electronic Publishing Industry Coalition™, is a global organization of published authors, publishers, editors, cover artists, and other industry professionals. EPIC was established as a strong voice for electronic publishing.

Literacy is close to the hearts of EPIC's members. In celebration of the new century, EPIC established the New Voices Young Writers Competition to encourage reading and writing among students ages 11 through 18, from public, private, or home-based schools.

This competition offers young writers an opportunity to learn about the versatility of eBooks and to experience a taste of the ePublishing world. It has promoted eBook awareness while inspiring young writers and poets to spread their wings and make their dreams reality.

Our children are not only the readers and writers of the future; they **are** the voice of the future.

EPIC has given that voice a place and time.

Here is that place.
Now is their time.

Come Fly with Us
and
Watch Dreams Unfold

The New Voices Writing Competition has experienced astounding success in its short history, receiving submissions from young writers from all over the globe.

Their stories, essays, and poems are judged according to high standards, and each entrant receives constructive feedback from our panel of published authors, publishers, editors, and education professionals. Their careful deliberation resulted in the winners which have been compiled in this anthology.

The satisfaction we receive in presenting these wonderful works for your enjoyment is matched by the joy we've had in choosing them.

TABLE OF CONTENTS

New Voices

GRAND PRIZE WINNERS

Junior Division
Grand Prize
and
First Place - Junior Division Essay

JiCi Wang
Kansas, USA

Picture the Music

I was standing outside the door with sheet music in my hands ready to be judged. It was a rainy Saturday afternoon. I was at Schmitt, a piano store, ready to play my three pieces for a piano competition.

"All right," said an older woman.

She was the judge's assistant, the one who tells the players when to come inside the room to be judged.

"Well come on, get ready," she urged.

I obediently followed. My heart was pounding heavily in my chest; my body was secretly shaking, but I wore a mask that was calm. Inside the room which was filled with organs, a young woman who was the judge sat behind a table with papers scattered all over it.

"Just hold on a moment," the judge added casually.

"All right," I replied, grateful she wasn't stiff and formal.

She smiled and went back to work. Her words and casualness put me at ease. I was no longer shaking, and my heart didn't pound as hard as before. After a moment, she looked up and gave me her full attention.

"Okay, you can begin."

I played through everything I was supposed to play. First my scales (a technique in piano), then my first

3

piece, and my second piece followed after that. The judge looked pleased. She said they were really good as I got ready to play my final piece. Suddenly, a subconscious voice inside me was urging me on, telling me to play this one extra well.

"Come on," I thought to myself, *"Think; make this special; make this the best you've ever done."*

I knew this piece (Mazurka in C major by Chopin) was written for a dance. It was slow, smooth, rather dreamy, and it had a lot of rubato (a term in music that means flexibility in tempo, sometimes slowing down or getting faster depending on what the pianist sees fit). I took a deep breath and began to play…

Suddenly I was no longer in the room filled with organs. Instead, I was playing in a large and elegant room with a marble floor. The world outside was dark and the lighting was dim. A dancer, dressed in pale blue, danced along with my music, her footsteps matching every note. At the quick trill towards the beginning of the piece, she did a quick turn. Effortless. Beautiful. Then my playing grew louder and louder, and her moves become big, **Huge!!!** *Rapidly the music became soft again, and so did the dancer. My playing became gentle, and then light. The dancer hopped, turned, and leaped as if she were a feather. Weightless. Graceful. My playing continued and the world became a blur around us. Our minds were focused on nothing but the music and the dance. Finally, the dancer stopped as I hit the last chord. Our performance was over.*

I was back in the organ room.

The judge looked up at me and said three words, "That was beautiful."

I thanked her, got up, and left the room.

On my way out of the store, I thought to myself, *"Anything, no matter how small or unimportant, even a simple piano piece can be special if you want it to be."*

Biography:
JiCi Wang was born in China in 1997 and came to the United States when she was seven years old. She started piano when she was eight and grew to love it. JiCi said, "Even thought there were times when I get really frustrated with my music, it's still worth learning the piano because I get to hear how much I improved and the wonderful music I'm making." Some of her favorite things to do are hanging out with her friends, listening to music, reading thrilling books, writing, and eating delicious food.

Commentary on eBooks:
"I honestly don't know what ePublishing or eBooks are. I just love writing so I occasionally write some essays and stories outside of school. My teacher recommended websites where I can find writing competitions where I can enter my works."

GRAND PRIZE WINNER
Senior Division
And
First Place - Senior Division Poetry

Laura Hoelzl
New York State, USA

Harbored

love is as love lives, here
in a tiny brown box squatting in the sand
bracing against splinters of wind and sea,
paint flakes cling determinedly to beaten posts
still supporting the warped walls
containing two tiny, wrinkled people
who have endured the elements as well
stooped but smiling
outsides betraying the hallmark of years
insides containing two selfless hearts
still tender and beating
showing no signs of slowing,
protected.

Biography:
Laura Hoelzl is a creative person who expresses herself through pencils and sneakers. She enjoys reading and writing, and is an avid runner. She hopes to one day see her work recognized, but not her name.

Commentary on eBooks:
"I have never personally used an eBook, but I find the idea fascinating. Combining what appear to be two incompatible fields, English and technology, ePublishing makes reading more convenient in a world where size and speed are vital. The gadget fiend is able to appreciate literature like never before."

JUNIOR POETRY

First Place

Meagan Kenney
Virginia, USA

Just A Sunrise...

Slowly rising from the ground
All is silent, not a sound
The first ray of light appears
Striking through the sky like spears
So many colors vibrant and bright
Finally the end of the night
Light's now leaking throughout the sky
The breeze blowing slowly by
The gentle warmth from the light
The brightness electrifying the sight
The smell of morning sweet and faint
Giving off a calmness you cannot taint
Beautiful enough to hypnotize
All of this from just a sunrise

~~~~

Biography:
Meagan is very interested in drama. She loves to sing, dance, and act. One day she would like to act professionally. Meagan also loves playing soccer and the piano in her spare time.

Commentary on eBooks:
"I actually haven't heard of eBooks and ePublishing, but they sound interesting. I hope to learn more about them in the future. I think it would be cool to learn about and use in school."

Second Place

Rose Baker
Virginia, USA

Shrouded for an Instant

I looked down from the top of a hill
on one cool September mid-morning.
Suddenly, I found myself placed in an
odd moment without warning.

While shrouded by an uncommon silence
I lost my sense of time.
The cars, the clothes were irrelevant
as I heard our changing culture rhyme.

I thought: *something seems to be*
the same as it was in a former century.
It could be how we form friendships;
but do too many facts oppose my theory?

Then came the inevitable:
my shroud was lifted.
Of course my efforts were in vain,
but I resisted.

Feeling pressured I have
continued with my modern ways.
But, a tiny part of my
mind continues this daze.

Biography:
Rose is an avid violinist. She also enjoys reading, playing soccer, and spending time with her friends. She has a little brother, an angelic dog, and a pesky cat.

Commentary on eBooks:
"I think that eBooks are a positive thing because they reach wider audiences. However, I personally prefer paper books because there is something special about printed words."

Third Place

Ryan Delaney
Kentucky, USA

Ode to my Five Year Old Brothers

I love my brothers so fun and wild.
They are the ones that make me smile.
They bounce off the walls like they live off caffeine.
They play lots of games that make me careen.

They are supposed to go to bed at eight,
But they always evade and stay up late.
They wake up so early the birds aren't up yet.
They wake me up so early that I often fret.

They always look out for each other in danger,
Like playing near traffic or meeting a stranger.
They always love doing new things,
Like playing instruments with strings.

They have as many friends
As hairs on their heads.
They always include the people left out,
So they can see people smile instead of pout.

My brothers are awesome.
My brothers are great.
You'd like them too,
If you had me to translate.

Biography:
Ryan loves to have fun, and plays football, soccer, and basketball. He loves doing plays and shows and hopes to make it to Broadway, Hollywood, or both. He also wants to be a politician. Ryan dislikes eating meat because he is a vegetarian. Ryan has twin 5 year-old brothers, who inspired his poem.

Commentary on eBooks:
"Although I do not have any experience with electronic books, they are a great idea. eBooks are compact so a person can carry millions of books on a very small device. This is also good for the environment since paper books use up lots of trees. Anyone could make an eBook and it would be easier to be published since the cost of making any number of copies of an eBook would be very small compared to printing a paper book."

Award of Excellence

Leila Graham
Pennsylvania, USA

Sometimes

Sometimes I wish upon a star,
But I can never wake up
Far away.
I want to disappear but I stay
Right where I am
As if nothing ever happened.

Sometimes I want to hide
And stay away,
Away from the outside world,
But I am always found.
And I never end up staying
Very long.

Sometimes I feel like I don't matter,
Like no one really cares.
Like I have disappeared for real.
And then and only then
I want to be found.
But at those times you
Are never there
For me.

Sometimes my door is closed
To you.
I don't want to see you,
Or hear you.
I don't want to deal with you.
I don't want to be near you,

Most of all,
I don't want to care about you,
But I do.

Sometimes you need to let me go,
Let me stay alone.
I will come to you when I am ready.
But until then,
I need to go on my own
And be my own person.

~~~~

Biography:
Leila likes writing poetry because it comes naturally and it's a way of expressing her feelings. She plays piano and particularly enjoys playing jazz. Her favorite school subject is history.

Commentary on eBooks:
"I think eBooks are great. I think they're a good invention but I don't want them to replace physical books. I like eBooks because they're lighter, easier to carry around when traveling and you can have lots of books in the space of one really small book."

Honorable Mention

Katie Ketterling
Idaho, USA

What Can I Do, What Can I Say?

What can I do, what can I say?
Why did it have to end this way?
I stay awake crying,
Knowing that my friend is dying.
As the days go by,
The more I start to cry.
I can't take this any longer.
For my weakness just keeps growing stronger.
What can I do, what can I say?
I wish this pain would just go away.
All the laughs, all the jokes we'd crack,
Knowing she's not coming back.
Tears run down my face,
Knowing I have lost something I can't replace.
For this I can't tell,
Because it feels like I'm under a spell.
What can I do, what can I say?
I guess all I can do now is pray.

~~~~

Biography:
Katie loves sports and her favorite food is chicken. She loves to sleep in. She's a class clown, always making you smile. She has three brothers and a sister. Changing schools a lot gives her a chance to make new friends.

Commentary on eBooks:
"I would love to find out about eBooks because I love to learn new things."

Judges' Award

Devika Chandramohan
California, USA

Yatra: A Journey

Come, let's run away.
Let the night cover our tracks.
Let the moon light up our path.
Let the whispers of the woods show us the way
On our pursuit for peace.

Come let's run away.
Let the wild beasts tame us.
Let the rain wash away our sins.
Let the smell of fresh dew cleanse our souls
On our pursuit for peace.

Come let's run away.
Let the twinkling stars teach us laughter.
Let the howling wind teach us sorrow.
Let the nesting bird teach us patience
On our pursuit for peace.

Come let's run away
And let nature take its course.

~~~~

Biography:
Devika is a regular thirteen-year-old with big dreams. She hopes to become a zoologist, writer, and teacher, but not all at the same time. She enjoys writing, reading, dancing, singing, playing with her hamster, and creating stories about strangers on the street. Devika looks up to her older brother as a role-model and a source of good humor. Though she's a serious student, she loves to laugh and goof around with her friends.

Commentary on eBooks:
"eBooks are the environmentally-friendly and convenient future of our normal bound books. These digital cousins of paper-bounds are already out in the market in products such as iPads and Kindles. They allow the community to read good books without having to cut down forests for paper, or burn fossil fuels to go to the library. Based on my experiences, I think eBooks are actually more fun to read than normal books. All the special effects added to the pages make it even cooler. I believe that in the future, all students will use eBooks instead of carrying heavy textbooks."

JUNIOR SHORT STORIES

First Place

Brady Achterberg
Pennsylvania, USA

The Watch

"It shows how long you have until you die," the girl had said.

Of course Mark Tewell hadn't believed it. He was just glad to get a new watch for free, and the little girl on the sidewalk had said she'd made one just for him. Even when he took a look at it and saw that it really was counting down, even when he saw (according to the watch) he had just ten months of life left before he keeled over, he thought it was broken and threw it in the junk drawer.

But now, there was only ten minutes left on the watch, and Mark Tewell was beginning to worry. *Suppose she was right?* This question bounced around his head over and over again. There was no possible way it could be true, but he still dreaded the moment the watch would hit zero. And of course, it didn't help that he was on vacation now, thirty feet from the sandy beach, at high tide, in water black as tar that was up to his waist and freezing him solid.

Mark rode a wave a bit closer to the beach and wondered again why he had brought the watch with him on the vacation. Until now, it had been kept in the bottom of the junk drawer, Mark only took it out to show to his snickering friends. But then he brought it along with him to the beach, just to watch it countdown to nada. Why? Had he *wanted* to get himself this nervous? He floated on the waves in thought.

A few waves more and he glanced at the watch again. Six minutes. He wondered if he should get out of the water, but he brushed the thought aside. He knew better than to let a broken watch scare *him* out of the water.

The tide was definitely coming in now. The waves towered over him and seemed to be trying to swallow him up. He looked at the watch. He now had just four minutes left until he "died." He moved in a little and readied himself for the next wave.

That wave was fine, but the one after crashed early and caught Mark unawares. Mark's boogeyboard slid out from under him and he came crashing down towards the sand. He raised one arm to keep his face from hitting, but the impact bent it at the wrong angle, and he came out of the water with one twisted arm.

Even a swimmer who doesn't think he'll die in four minutes wouldn't dare stay in the water with a useless arm. He walked out onto the beach and lay down on his towel, gasping for breath. He bent his arm up painfully to look at the time.

The watch was gone.

He looked at his wrist in astonishment. It must have fallen off when he hurt his arm! Like an idiot, Mark sprinted back into the water to see where it went. He felt it on the seafloor.

The watch was being chased by the tide out to the coral reef, and Mark Tewell swam after it, holding his breath. The watch tumbled in to a tiny hole in the coral. Mark stuck his hand in and found the watch about six inches in. He slipped his hand right into the watch and pulled it around his wrist. Then he tried to pull his hand back out.

It was stuck. With the watch attached, his hand was too big to pull out of the coral. He tried pulling it off his hand, but he found that it was stuck tight. He was trapped and couldn't hold his breath for much longer. Violently, he tried to wrench his arm out of the reef, but the coral was like stone.

With two minutes left on the watch, Mark Tewell lost consciousness.

Later

The lifeguard on the beach had been keeping an eye on Mark Tewell. He'd seen him hurt his arm and had wondered why he was swimming back out in that condition. Now he was swimming through the water to learn why he hadn't come back in almost four minutes.

He found him and pulled his hand out violently, breaking the watch off. Then he swam back to shore and began CPR. It took a full minute, but eventually Mark came back, and was rushed to the hospital.

Mark Tewell lived a full life and never looked for the watch again.

~~~~

Biography:
Brady Achterberg is the oldest of three children and lives on a small farm with his thirty-two individually named chickens. His hobbies are soccer, fencing, and the game D&D. In his spare time, he reads, chases chickens, and attempts to communicate with his small and brainless dog.

Commentary on eBooks:
"eBooks and ePublishing have everything going for them. Reading with Kindle and other eBooks is faster, cheaper, greener, and more helpful than book. The only statement in defense of paper-bound books is that people like the "feel" of paper. Still, Kindle will never replace traditional books because books have a certain authentic quality that eBooks don't have."

Second Place

Katie Morse
Virginia, USA

The F.F.P.
(Fairy Follow Program)

"Petal "

"Here!" I said, when Mr. Leaf called my name. I'm in the Fairy Follow Program, F.F.P. for short. I'm only eleven years old, but my parents make me participate in it. I just want to be a normal fairy who gets up and goes to school. My family has been participating in this program for years. You follow a human that doesn't believe in fairies, and give them signs that there is a fairy nearby so they start to believe.

"I'll give you a slip of paper with your human's name, age, and where they go to school." Mr. Leaf instructed. As he passed out the papers, I heard fairies groan. Only a few of them cheered. This scared me. I finally got my slip of paper. It said:

Savannah Patterson, River Bank Middle
Age: 12

I was scared about my assignment, but I knew I would feel great after accomplishing it.

The next day, I flew into River Bank Middle.

"Let's see," I told myself. "A 12-year-old would be in 6th grade."

" Vannah! Wait up!" A girl with black hair and thick brown glasses called to another girl.

"Hey!" I yelled. I saw the girl I was looking for! I followed her into a classroom. On the chalkboard,

26

someone had written: *Mr. Hall, 6ᵗʰ Grade History*

"Hi, Lizzie!" Savannah told the girl with glasses.

"Vannah! There is a fairy here! I know it! I met one when I was little, and I have a strange feeling there's one here now."

I flew under a chair. I didn't like humans, especially suspicious ones.

"Oh Man!" Savannah yelled. "Fairies aren't–"

She stopped yelling when a boy with blonde hair, green eyes, and braces walked in. She had this look on her face that reminded me of what my Aunt Rose looked like at her wedding. This must be Savannah's true love. I didn't waste any time. I pulled out a bag of fairy dust, and sprinkled it on the boy.

No one seemed to notice. I closed the door that separated the classroom from their Super Student Corner. There were 3 butterfly chairs, 2 board games, and a TV. I guess good students got to rest in here. This was a great place to talk privately.

"Whoa! You're a ..." the boy started.

"I know!" I yelled. "What's your name?"

"Jason, but –"

"I'm Petal! I need a favor."

"Please stop interrupting me!"

"Savannah Patterson really likes you. I need her to believe in fairies. It's my job. Help me convince her we are real! I'll fly around, and see if she notices my fairy dust. Then, I'll start to clap to see if she hears me. If that fails, then you must tell her."

Jason agreed to help, but would my plan work?

I had to wait an hour, and listen to a lesson about cells, but it was worth it. The bell rang and Savannah, Lizzie, and Jason were the first ones in. I came in after them. Savannah sat in the front next to Jason.

"Show time!" I told myself. I flew around in front of her. Lizzie watched from her seat.

"Vannah! It's a fairy. See for yourself!" Lizzie was excited.

"It's probably just the wind blowing glitter around."

This wasn't going to work. I started clapping, while singing obnoxiously.

"I hear her!" Lizzie was enjoying all of this.

"It's just someone in the hallway!" Savannah was fed up. "I don't believe in fairies."

"Help!" I yelled to Jason.

"Um, Savannah, I met a fairy last period. They are real."

I flew down to the table, and sat next to Jason and Savannah.

"Savannah, I'm Petal. I work for the Fairy Follow Program. I follow a human who doesn't believe, and give them clues so they do believe." I ended with a sigh. I hate talking to humans. You have to yell for them to hear you.

Savannah looked surprised. "I'm so sorry! From now on, I'll always believe!"

I was happy to be successful with my mission. I was tired, but excited to get back to Mr. Leaf and let him know one more human believed.

"Petal, here is your grade." Mr. Leaf handed me a piece of paper. I was so scared. This is what the paper said: Mission Grade: A Good Job! Mr. Leaf.

~~~

Biography:
Katie loves writing and has a great imagination.

Commentary on eBooks:
I would like to publish a book of my own one day. Maybe I will try ePublishing.

Third Place

Jennifer Xu
Ontario, Canada

Flightless

I looked up at the October sky, which was filled with dark grey clouds covering the remaining bits of sunlight. Just the way I felt every day, oppressed by ominous thoughts like a big rain cloud hanging over me. I wondered what my friend was doing right now. Two years ago, at the age of 11, I had been unofficially homeless and hungry. Alexis, who was 13 at that time, had helped me, taught me the basics of survival and soon enough, we became friends. As I ran these memories over in my head, a voice spoke.

"Did you get it?"

It was Alexis, back from a "shopping spree." I felt around the pockets of my tattered jacket and pulled out a pocket watch. As she examined it, she handed over two small loaves of bread. Stale of course, but I wolfed them down anyway. Although we were friends, when it came down to this, we were businesswomen, careful of our purchases and sales.

"Nice job, Hope." Alexis commented. "This can get us quite a bit of money from the pawnshop."

I looked up at her and smiled. Then, quick as a rabbit, she changed back to friend mode.

"Have you ever thought about birds?" she asked almost dreamily.

"What? We have nowhere to stay, we're always hungry and we might be caught by cops one day and you're thinking about birds?!?!" I asked incredibly.

"I didn't mean it that way! What I'm trying to say is that birds always seem to be free, not a care in the world, no hunger and best of all, a home to go home to anywhere, anytime. Not only this, they soar over the clouds watching over us." Alexis sighed contently.

"And sometimes, they poop on us and we need to find somewhere to wash our clothes!" I retorted.

"Thank you so much for ruining my moment." Alexis said sarcastically.

"You're welcome." I answered in the same tone.

After a moment of semi-awkward silence, I pulled out a beaten up mattress from behind the dumpster and a dingy old quilt from under a cardboard box.

"Good night, Hope."

"Good night, Alexis."

I drifted off to sleep.

When I woke up the next morning, I noticed that Alexis was gone. I started to worry. Usually, Alexis would wait for me to get up before she leaves. I sprung up, hastily hiding everything and set out to find her. She wasn't in the pawnshop, the bakery or the bank. I walked for at least half an hour and still didn't see her.

And then I did.

Alexis was lying on her back on the side of the road. I rushed over to her and examined her. No pulse, no breathing. Just icy cold hands. I started to shake. I'm not sure how long I was there, I just remember telling her to stay alive even though in my heart, I knew she was gone.

When I finally composed myself, I checked her pockets. Inside was $50.00, from the trade of the pocket watch. Nothing else was with her. I stood up, took one last look at her, and ran off.

Back at the alleyway, I thought about everything we've through, from two years ago to now. I lost track of time. The overcast sky turned from light grey to dark grey seemingly in a matter of minutes. I only realized it when I found myself hungry and cold.

I raced to the bakery and peered into the window.

Closed.

Now I could act. I pulled out a lock picking set given to me from Alexis for my birthday last year. I almost turned to remind her of that until I recalled that I'll never talk to her again. I sighed and got to work. A jiggle to the left, now the right, and twist. Awesome. I was in.

I sprinted inside, grabbed as many loaves of bread as I could take, slapped about $20.00 on the table and ran out, locking the door behind me. I ran back to my abode, eating along the way.

As I got ready for bed, the thought of no Alexis crashed down on me. I cried myself to sleep and dreamt. I dreamt about food, shelter and love. I dreamt about playing a video game like all the normal kids. But most vivid of all, I dreamt about Alexis and I, hand in hand, soaring free as birds over the clouds that have shadowed me for so long.

~~~~

Biography:
Jennifer strives for perfection and keeps her locker and school binder neat. She has a dolphin obsession; they're everywhere in her room and she likes talking about them. She has a little brother who is in the "I will talk as loudly as I want" stage at the age of four.

Commentary on eBooks:
"eBooks are useful and nice to carry with you because they aren't as heavy as the "traditional" hardcover/soft cover books. In addition, you can download all kinds of stories from websites for a cheaper price than buying them. The only downside is, if you have a slow computer, it'll take a while to just download a page."

Award of Excellence

Sarah Parris
South Carolina, USA

Miracle Place

On the way through the woods to her Miracle Place, Wendy heard her favorite sounds: birds chirping, leaves crunching, and trees swaying in the cool breeze. Wendy was headed for her Miracle Place, the place that she talked to God and relaxed. That was almost the only place Wendy could escape her brother.

Wendy, just eleven years old, had been adopted by an older couple along with her biological brother, Sam. Sam had a brain tumor and as the doctors estimated had less than three months to live. Wendy needed her Miracle Place to talk to God and plead with him to heal her brother. Wendy's mind was filled with questions like: why my brother, he's only five? Wendy had already asked every grown up she knew, but no one could answer her questions, except God.

"God," Wendy prayed, "why are you letting this happen? Please answer the questions I have that nobody else can answer." Tears welled up in her eyes just even thinking about what it would be like without Sam.

"Clang, clang, clang." Her adopted mother rang a bell which Wendy thought could probably be heard on the moon. Wendy hesitated before leaving her Miracle Place.

"Please God," Wendy prayed while she walked on toward a warm meal, a house, her family and life.

Wendy, surprised to see the pastor's car in the driveway, jogged the rest of the way to the house. When she walked in, her parents were both crying and the pastor looked like he was about to do the same.

"What's wrong?" Wendy asked.

Her mother mumbled something, and then the pastor spoke up.

"It's Sam, Wendy."

Wendy's mind was filled with thoughts: he had been kidnapped, he had run away, he was lost, but never once did what the pastor was about to say pass through her mind.

"He died."

"What, this can't be," Wendy snapped. "How did it happen?" Wendy said, calming down.

"His brain tumor caused it, his body just couldn't handle that much pain," the pastor answered.

Before Wendy knew what was happening she was tearing through the woods straight toward her Miracle Place.

"No, God, no. Why did it have to happen?"

Tears flooded down her cheeks. She reached her Miracle Place and stopped and thought, just 30 minutes ago I was here to try to escape my brother and now he is dead.

"I didn't even get to say goodbye to him God, why did you let him die?"

Then a loud voice bellowed, "Wendy, he came home." It was God, she knew it. "Wendy, because he's a Christian he came up here with us and is having a good time and he's not in pain," the voice said.

"But why?" Wendy asked.

"So his death could lead you to me," the loud voice answered, "be my child Wendy."

Suddenly, Wendy realized she really did need God, a savior, her savior. Right in her Miracle Place Wendy accepted Jesus Christ as her Savior and Lord! "Thanks God, and thanks Sam."

Biography:
Sarah loves playing sports and writing. Her favorite
sports are: volleyball, basketball and horseback riding.
Horses are her favorite animal. She has two older sisters.

Commentary on eBooks:
I don't know much about ePublishing. I use the Internet
both for pleasure and school work. We research things in
history and science on the Internet and I also use it for
current events sometimes.

Honorable Mention

Bessie Liu
California, USA

Confessions

"Here, Katie," the librarian smiled, handing me a small blue bookmark. I took it happily, unaware that this bookmark would change the entire rest of my third grade year. All I cared about at that moment was that the dancing penguin was extremely cute.

Over the next few months, I lost track of the bookmark, but noticed one of my classmates, Sofya, edging farther away from me. Bewildered, I wondered why. Had we ever fought? Had she hated me before? These were questions I could not answer, as the days dragged by.

Then, one day, I brought to school a book I had long since abandoned, and flipped to the page where I'd left off. There sat my faithful penguin bookmark. I was seized by a sudden whim to find out how many other bookmarks had remained loyal to their owners.

"Katie, do you want to play?" the voice of my best friend, Natasha, echoed in my ear.

"Sorry, Natasha, but I just want to check on a few things," I burst out. I felt a twinge of guilt when Natasha nodded and backed out of the classroom.

I began by scouring the desktops of every student. There was no penguin in sight. As I turned my search towards the insides of the desks, I noticed with a jolt that I wasn't alone in the room. Another girl was sitting at her table, watching me with disapproving brown eyes. Oh no! Sofya had seen me probing the room for the bookmarks.

At first I felt surprised, then angry and embarrassed

35

that my plan had failed after all, so that I barely registered a blue piece of paper sticking out from the book she was leafing through. It was her penguin bookmark! A new idea sparked in my mind. Gripping mine more tightly, I stepped boldly toward her. Her aloof expression softened into curiosity and caution.

"Do you want to be friends?"

I could almost visualize her hair bristling in indignation. But the only thing she said was, "Uh...why?"

She doesn't want to, I thought wildly. Forcing myself to keep my head, I continued, "Because my bookmark is lonely. She wants someone to play with. And I know you have the same bookmark." This plea sounded like something a toddler would say, but I could not think of any other way to convince Sofya that accepting my friend request would be worthwhile.

"Okay...sure. But I'm sure that other people have these bookmarks too..."

Sweeping my arm toward the clusters of desks, I explained, "Actually, they don't. A lot of people threw them away. The rest of them who kept theirs tore them up." This was probably true, but right now I didn't really care about being honest.

Sofya's frown curled into a smile.

The next few days slipped by with blissful quickness, but still unease lurked. I had to find out why Sofya had been avoiding me in the past few months. And you wouldn't believe how easily the story unfolded.

We had encountered each other in second grade when our classes merged for reading time. "I remember thinking 'Oh, I'll never be friends with that girl'," Sofya joked, but seeing my serious expression, she added, "Oh, come on, Katie! You know I didn't know you well in second grade."

"Yes, never mind," I said hastily. "Go on."

In second grade, she had planned to become friends with Natasha. "I was so jealous of you because you stole her." My stomach lurched when she told me that.

Towards the middle of third grade, the whole class had been given those bookmarks. Sofya explained that her friend had stolen her penguin bookmark, which she had stolen back. To watch me snooping around the room must have been like a glimpse back in time for her, I realized with a pang of remorse.

Suddenly, Sofya surprised me again by standing up quickly. "I hope you'll still be my friend after this," she pleaded earnestly, her brown eyes searching mine. But I needed no persuasion. My mind was made up.

In a whirlwind of activity, third grade swept past, and to this day, we are still best friends.

If I ever feel like something in my life's messed up, I just glance at my bookmark, marveling at how the warmth seeps back into my body whenever I recall the special link between my best friend and me.

~~~~

Biography:
Bessie Liu wants to be a doctor or writer when she grows up. She plays viola and piano, and paints as well. Bessie's favorite memory is writing her first short story in elementary school. She enjoys the Pets and Health section of Yahoo!Answers, and online news.

Commentary on eBooks:
"I used an eBook at Google Books, and the experience was great! My teacher assigned search for 'To Build A Fire' by Jack London online. I went to Google Books and found a perfect version of the short story. I would recommend Google Books and eBooks to other people."

Judges' Award

Hayley Gompertz
California, USA

Forever Forest

It is an unwritten rule among the people living around the Forever Forest to never stray from the main trail, for if they do, no one will ever see them again.

Ever.

However, a foolish, young traveler, ignorant of this rule, entered the forest, following the path until he heard something.

"Somebody! Somebody! Help! I'm stuck in a tree!" a girl called.

The traveler looked around for the source. "Where are you then? I can't tell where you are."

"Left and then go straight. I'm stuck in a tree!" The boy looked left; a bramble blocked his view.

Thoughtlessly, he dropped his bags and made his way through the bush, leaving the path.

"Please hurry, traveler!" He stumbled mindlessly through the forest, imagining the girl's appearance: A girl wearing the clothes of a runaway child, with brown hair, pale skin and round, blue eyes.

He tripped over a dead log, the image of her blocking his vision.

"You are almost here, hurry."

The boy righted himself on a tree starting his trek again, following her voice, which sounded like it came from twelve different directions.

"Where are you?" The traveler called out to the girl, holding his chest.

"A little farther, hurry!"

Some of the cuts on his hands and face bled, caused

by the bushes. Despite this, he went on, yearning for the girl.

She sat in a tree where the branches split apart to leave room for her body as she clutched one of the thicker branches. She held a sunflower stalk.

She had long black hair curling around her face, her eyes an emerald green, and wore a dainty dress. She could have been twelve or thirteen.

"Thank you for coming to help. I'm afraid I can't get off. And I'm frightened."

"I'll help you." The boy helped her down, setting her on her feet, his gaze drawn to her.

She straightened and stood dusting herself down. "Thank you so much. Shall we take a walk?" She ambled away when he nodded his head and followed her like a baby duck.

The traveler caught up to her and she grabbed his hand. "I want to show you something that has not been seen by anyone in a long time." The girl brought the traveler to a clearing. "Nobody goes this deep into the forest so nobody can see this wonderful garden."

The garden had various plants. However, only about half of the plot was filled. Each plant was different. He saw a sunflower, a lily, a daffodil, and a rose.

"What is the design? Any pattern?" he asked.

"What is your favorite flower?" she asked stroking a tall bushy plant. "That is its pattern. So what is your favorite flower?"

The boy thought for a second. "I like carnations."

The girl nodded and pulled a packet of seeds from her pocket. "Can you plant it for me?"

He held his hand out to receive the packet. "Of course I will." She dropped the package into his hands.

He walked to an empty spot and knelt. He poured the package into a hole he dug. Patting the hole, he stood, turning back to her. "I'm finished. Except, it needs water."

She stood smiling. "Tell me a little about yourself, traveler."

He rubbed his chin in thought. "Well my name is Anthony, from the town of Hillfoot, and I'm a fifteen years old. What about you?"

"My name," she said with a singsong voice, "is Belial. I've lived in this forest since *forever*." She took a step closer to him. "So what brought you through the forest?"

He thought. Why was he here? He took a while remembering.

"I came through the forest to visit the town on the other side. My girlfriend lives there." A thought struck him. "And I have to be there by two days time!" He flinched and looked around, worried. He'd left the path and forgotten how to get back to the main trail.

She frowned. "Why would you like her over me? We can live together forever by this beautiful garden."

"I have to-" The girl wrapped her arms around him.

"What would I do if I get stuck again? Don't you want to make sure I'm safe?" She clung to his body and the boy's mind went blank.

The girl sat in a tree, smelling a red carnation. "Somebody! Somebody! Help! I'm stuck in a tree!"

Biography:
Hayley's main interests are writing, drawing and anime. She loves to play her favorite characters, as well as drawing them and writing fan fiction about them. She also enjoys spending time with her friends, family and her dog, Macy.

Commentary on eBooks:
"Most of my experience with eBooks is through fan fiction that's posted on the web at various sites. I write my stories using Word, then post them to the sites, a chapter at a time. I'm very interested in pursuing a career in graphic arts, perhaps making cover art for eBooks, and also in writing them."

JUNIOR ESSAYS

Second Place

Javan Latson
Florida, USA

A Rose That Was Formed By a Tear

Gather round and you shall hear
Of a rose that was formed
By a dreadful tear.

Oh the Cherokees sadly made their way,
But in their hearts they wanted to stay
As they walked that trail
They remembered the day
When the government sent them
On a journey far, far away.

In the year 1838, thousands of Cherokee were forced on a journey from their homes in the mountains of North Georgia onto reservations in Oklahoma. Many died along this journey that became known as the "Trail of Tears." The Cherokee call it the "Place Where They Cried."

Being forced to leave their homes without notice was a painful experience. Ancestral lands were important to the Cherokee. As the women marched on their journey, they wept. The men quarreled and fought one another. Sometimes, they even killed each other. The lack of nutritious food and the harsh environment was more than some of the children could endure. The women cried because they were unable to feed their children. Many perished.

With so much death and sadness the clan elders

prayed to God. They asked Him if He would do something to lift their spirits. God's answer was to give them a sign. The sign was a rose. Everywhere a tear was shed, a rose would grow as a testimony to the valiant people of the Cherokee nation who made this journey.

The rose was white with a gold center and seven leaves. The white color symbolized the women's tears of grief. The gold center represented the gold that had been stolen from them when they were forced to leave Georgia. The seven leaves represented the seven Cherokee lands. Amazingly, this rose flourished all along the trail. Everywhere a tear had fallen from the face of a Cherokee on this march a rose bloomed as an everlasting sign of encouragement.

More than a hundred years have passed since the Cherokee took their journey. Yet, the beautiful Cherokee rose still blooms wild along the route known as the "Trail of Tears." Ironically, the State of Georgia that cast out the Cherokee people from its northern mountains decided to adopt the Cherokee Rose as its state flower in 1916. To this day, we recognize this beautiful flower as the rose that was formed by tears.

~~~~

Biography:
Javan loves fun in the sun playing a variety of sports, especially basketball. He is an animal lover with a pair of leopard geckoes, two dogs, and a dwarf rabbit as pets. His dream is to become a medical doctor who plays professional basketball. His favorite subjects are science and history.

Commentary on eBooks:
I have accessed a number of eBooks on my iPod. I think being able to access literary works electronically is great.

Third Place

Lara Taniguchi
Osaka Prefecture, Japan

Samurai vs. Knight

Medieval Europe lasted from approximately 500 AD to 1000 AD, while Feudal Japan lasted from approximately 552 AD to 1854 .D. There were many differences between the two places. Though they were halfway around the world from each other, and did not have much technology to communicate, similarities could be found in the government and hierarchy system.

There were several similarities that were all related to government structure. In Medieval Europe, the king was at the top of the social hierarchy and in Feudal Japan the emperor was at the top. Although they held the highest ranking, both had no real power to control people, while the landowners, for example the lords and daimyo, gained lots of power to govern.

In both places there were strong military leaders such as the officials and shogun. The lords and daimyo similarly had peasants working for them by farming crops on their land. In exchange they gave the peasants land and protection. Adding to that, farming was also the main economic activity in both Japan and Europe.

Along with the peasants, professionally trained soldiers worked for the landowners. They were required to protect the landowners and their territory. In Europe, these soldiers were called knights, and in Japan they were called samurai. Both types of soldiers were requested to follow a code of honor. The samurai followed Bushido which called for honor, loyalty, and bravery.

The main principle of Bushido was Zen. The knights

were expected to live by chivalry in which they were supposed to be deeply religious and defend the Catholic Church. They were expected to protect the women and the weak and be brave in battle. They also had to fight against injustice. The skills of the knights and samurai were greatly valued because both had a high rank in society and were respected.

Some differences between Feudal Japan and Medieval Europe include literature, religion, women's rights, education, and clean surroundings. The literature, such as poetry, was different. In Feudal Japan, the haiku was popular. It was short and usually described nature. In contrast to that, the epic poem was popular in Medieval Europe. It was very long and mostly about warriors or heroes. Lyric poems were also popular and were sung like songs. In addition, the religions were different as well. The knights believed in Christianity while the samurai believed in Shinto and Zen.

Besides the first two differences, the social position of women in Japan and Europe were unalike. In Japan, the women had a more equal status with men. They could inherit property and they could also make choices about their future. They also had the responsibility to protect their home if their samurai husbands were at war. On the other hand, the rights of the women in Europe were limited. They had to marry the man chosen for them, and they were also expected to do house chores.

Another difference was that education was more valued to the Japanese compared to the Europeans. In Japan, especially during the isolation period, there were not many enemies, so there was time and resources for education. Yet in Europe, there were many wars so it was logical to train to become a knight rather than wasting time to study. Finally, Japan had more sanitary surroundings compared to Europe. In Europe, people even threw their toilet waste out the window.

In conclusion, living in Feudal Japan would be better than living in Medieval Europe. There are several reasons why.

First of all, as a woman, you could have a more of an equal status as men. You could decide your future unlike in Medieval Europe where even your husband was chosen for you. I would have liked to live in Japan in cleaner surroundings. Feudal Japan may have some things that don't give a good impression on living there. However, I think it would be best to live in a peaceful environment.

Lastly, in Medieval Europe and Feudal Japan, regardless of all the differences and the lack of technology and other advancements, they were common in many ways. Adding to that, at this moment in time, there were distinctive differences, such as culture and religion, which were developed during many years between Europe and Japan. However, the two places carry a considerable number of similarities and are tightly linked because of advanced technology and other modern developments.

~~~~

Biography:
Lara Taniguchi loves reading, and her favorite book is **The Hunger Games**. She's a violinist and ballet dancer, and swims, plays tennis and Ultimate Frisbee. Cooking is one of her hobbies, and she invents new recipes. She loves traveling, especially booking the airplane tickets and packing her suitcases.

Commentary on eBooks:
"I think eBooks are such an amazing invention, because you can download books onto your eReader instantly. This is great when you are at airport and are bored. I didn't really know much about eBooks until I got an iPad! Now I am obsessed with reading eBooks on it."

Award of Excellence

Estelle Baldwin
Connecticut, USA

Sweden to Me

To me, I feel like Sweden isn't just the place that my mom is from. I feel like it is my second home. Everyone has a special place or hometown, but for me Sweden is different.

I feel like I'm welcome there since practically all of my mom's side of the family lives there. I feel independent when I tell my mom that I'll go bike to the store to get more milk. Everything is so local in Torekov, Sweden, compared to Connecticut, so we always bike places instead of driving a car. We only use a car if we are going somewhere far, or to the airport with luggage. There are open fields, and livestock such as cows, sheep, horses, and more everywhere you look, and everyone is friendly. Whenever I get on my bike, and have the wind blow in my face with the sun beaming down on me, I feel free.

Whenever I look back or think about Torekov, I have a happy feeling inside me. When I get to Torekov in the summer, I feel like a different me. I feel grown-up when I can go hang out with a friend after dinner, or go mini-golfing with my cousins. I can meet up with a friend and go play tennis or go to an ice-cream shop, or a candy shop. You never get bored there because there is always something to do with a friend, or somewhere to go. I love Sweden because I can choose with my friend Matildia if we want to speak Swedish or English. I help her speak English and she helps me speak Swedish.

Sweden is a place where I can reveal the inner me. I

can reveal a different side of me without having to worry about what people might think. I can be myself instead of trying to blend in with everyone else. In Connecticut, I have to worry about what brand of clothes I wear, and I have to worry about what toy is "in" so my friends don't think I am weird. In Sweden I don't have to worry about those things. I can wear what I want, and do what I want and everyone accepts me for who I am.

I feel special when I go to Sweden. Every morning that I wake up in Sweden, I can smell the coffee that my parents and grandparents are drinking, and the eggs my grandma is cooking as they sizzle on the pan. I can hear the waves crashing on the shore since we live right off the coast in a big white house. Almost every morning I wake up to sunlight which makes me want to get up and get outside. There are all different sizes of bikes lined up along the side of the house just ready to take me somewhere.

Our family has a tradition of going to Sweden every year in the summer. Every summer I look forward to going there. I get to see my cousins, my grandparents, and my godmother. I have such good memories from Sweden and the people there. Like the time when I was a flower girl for my godmother's sister's wedding. I can picture my godmother walking beside me, clenching my hand because both of us were so nervous. I have one bad memory from Sweden though. That was when my grandma woke me up and told me that my brother James was in the hospital because he had fallen off his bike. This might not seem too bad, but he got a cut the size of a loaf of bread on his shoulder and a concussion.

Sweden is very important to my family, because it is practically half of us. What I mean by that is that my mom is Swedish, but my dad is American. Since practically the whole side of my mom's side of the family lives there, Sweden is a special place for my family. My grandma's sister lives right down the street from where we stay, so my cousins and I bike down there to see my grandma's sisters, daughters, baby named Ella. Ella is my godmother's sister's baby. I'm excited to see Ella's new sister, Lisa, this summer.

I can easily picture everything on our street in Torekov since I've been going there for all my life. For example, there is this one part of the street where there is a half-circle like place, where the street has two ways for you to go. You can keep going straight, or you can go in the half-circle way. There is this "island" in the center of the half-circle where there is this one long bush where the bunnies hide when my cousins and I look for them. We could never catch them because they are way too fast for us. We watch them hop away with their white fluffy tails behind them.

I love Sweden, and the good memories from Torekov. I look forward to going to Sweden every summer. I've been going to Sweden every single summer of my life and that's a tradition I never want to break.

~~~~~

Biography:
Estelle Baldwin has lived in the USA for her whole life, but her mother is Swedish. Her favorite sports are gymnastics and soccer. Estelle has two dogs which she loves very much. Estelle spends her free time with friends and family and loves being active outdoors.

Commentary on eBooks:
I have never had any experience with eBooks but I am sure I would enjoy them.

Honorable Mention

Arshiya Ansari
Virginia, USA

Details Matter the Most

When I listen to a song the lyrics matter the most for me. In the same way, the details matter the most in life. Laughing with your friends, or just taking a walk on a cool summer's day are far better than fancy cars, classy homes, and stylish clothes. When you accomplish something and the smile that spreads across your face fills you up with happiness, that's what matters the most. Details, the small things in life are the ones that bring you satisfaction whether it's helping someone in need or the excitement of presents on Christmas morning. So many things in life matter but I feel that friends, family and memories are the three main topics that everyone can relate to.

Every day I see my friends and I can't help but smile. There's a special feeling when you're with friends who really care for you, they complete your thoughts and you can *always* count on them! You remember everything they tell you and they'll listen to your stories as well, you can act like your own dorky self when they're around. You can discuss anything with them; trust them with all your secrets knowing that they will never tell anyone, that's what true friends act like. If we didn't have friends then the delicate fabric which we call life will slowly unthread.

Your family cares for you, your family supports you but at times you may feel like you want to be anywhere else than with them. It's true that our family members can be a pain but inside they really care for you. I feel that life without your Mom's warm, comforting words or your Dad's husky hug or even your siblings' constant complaining could result in a very gloomy world. When you're scared, who's there to comfort you? When you're sad, who's there to cheer you up? The answer to both these questions is your family. Your family deals with everything you give them and you'll have to deal with everything they give you as well but life without your family is unthinkable.

Memories are like mini movies that play over and over in your head but they're close to your heart and you'll never get tired of them. You'll remember when you first rode your bike without training wheels, you'll remember when you got your very first friend and you'll also remember some negative memories but without them how would you realize that your life isn't perfect and that you should keep trying to work harder? Your friends' and family members' faces will flip through your head and you'll remember each and every moment you spent with them, the good or the bad because without memories will you remember anything? One day you'll look back at your life and say, "I remember the time I did this..." and you'll feel so good about it. Memories are the contentment of your life.

Just think about life without friends, family, and memories to look back upon of all the good times you've had. It is unimaginable because you'll have to depend on yourself and no one will care for you. These aren't the important details in life, there are many more but I feel life without these three would be horrible. Details really do matter the most, because everybody could experience friends, family and memories but could you experience fancy cars, classy homes, and stylish clothes? Not everyone could and details are more important than the big things in life. Details are sewn everywhere in the fabric that's called life.

Biography:
Arshiya Ansari is creative beyond expectations. She is always writing, no matter what. She never disappoints anyone and is always on task. Whether Arshiya is writing for an assignment or just for fun, she always writes with the same passion. Arshiya also likes to play sports like basketball and tennis. She spends a lot of time in the local library, reading and learning. Arshiya never wants to stop learning and she always takes criticism well. She is an excellent student and she loves to write, read, and learn.

Commentary on eBooks:
"I do not prefer eBooks. For me to enjoy a book, I have to hold it. I have to feel the pages with the words printed on them. I have to stay up to the latest hour just so I can finish reading a chapter under a proper light. To me eBooks dehumanize books. eBooks make you strain more than you have to.

"But eBooks have their pros. Like the different variety of books you can get off the Internet. eBooks also are quicker, as in the wait. The wait for a book is very long, especially if the book is high in demand. It makes reading faster. But still the wait is worthwhile when you read an amazing book."

Judges' Award

Bessie Liu
California, USA

The Pool of Golden Pebbles

I don't know what made me walk toward that still pool of water; all I knew was that the cruise to Mexico had not been much fun. That's probably why I was excited about my chance to go to that evening party. But if I had known what was about to happen in the next hour, I would have asked my parents to let me stay behind.

As soon as I stepped into the vast room, with windows that stretched to the ceiling and a floor of polished marble, I knew that this night would be unusual. I followed my family around the ballroom, jazzy music blaring in my ears. That's when I glimpsed the pond.

It was a shining expanse of crystal clear water. Gazing into its depths, I noticed a pile of golden pebbles lying at the bottom. I stroked one of the smooth rocks, thinking of bringing one back as a souvenir. I turned around and opened my mouth to tell my mom...but she wasn't there!

Wildly searching the room, which was quickly filling up with people, I began to realize the truth: my parents had deserted me! Stumbling toward the crowd, I shrieked, "Mom?" No answer. Panic erupted inside of me. As I wandered through the crowd in search of my family, I stared at every single person I passed. None of them looked like my mom, dad, or little sister. Bewildered and angry, I felt the tears slowly start to well up.

I floundered toward the platform where the musicians

were playing. A wave of pain struck me as I remembered how I had longed to learn a new instrument. Would I ever get the chance now?

"Excuse me, are you lost?"

I felt a hand on my shoulder, and looked up into the concerned face of the pianist, darkened by anxiety. Her hair was as black as my mom's, and she was wearing glittery clothing. There was sympathy in her eyes.

Shame crept up on me, as I turned myself away from her offer of help. I did not need someone else's pity; I needed to find my parents! Then, I noticed that I was perched on a piano chair. I remember staring around with teary eyes while the pianist asked the whole room whose child I was.

There were so many faces! Some looked interested, while others seemed unconcerned. I could feel one thought running through every child in that room: *I'm so glad that's not me!* The lights, instead of gleaming a warm yellow, were now flashing mocking colors of blue and purple. They must all have been laughing at me. I still cannot remember being more indignant than then, when I realized that this whole room was against me.

Then, in a far corner, I heard a shout, "Hey, that's Bessie!" My parents were standing in that far corner, looking utterly embarrassed to see the problem being addressed to everyone in the party room.

Ha, they deserve it, I told myself angrily. But then, I gazed at my baby sister, Katie. Her eyes glanced up at me with pure innocence, as if she was wondering why I was displayed on a stage when she was in my mom's arms. Looking at her changed my attitude, and convinced me that it was not my family's fault that we were being humiliated.

Walking down the steps of the stage took me out of the spotlight. I hurried toward my mom, dad, and sister. As I neared my parents, who seemed to be trying hard not to laugh, their hands reached forth to pull me towards safety and security. I turned to say something to the pianist, but she had vanished.

Now I tell somebody where I'm going or what I'm going to do before actually doing it. I also learned that when it comes to the real world, I am not so independent as everybody usually thinks. But that's okay – there are people who will care for you. That pianist went out of her way to help me. And yet, she slipped out of my life that evening, as if she had never existed. I wish I could have thanked her.

~~~~

Biography:
Bessie Liu is interested in becoming a doctor or writer when she grows up. She plays the viola and piano, and likes to paint as well. Bessie's favorite memory is of writing her first fictionalized short story in elementary school. She enjoys going to the Pets and Health section of Yahoo!Answers, and checking on the news online.

Commentary on eBooks:
"I used an eBook at Google Books once, and the experience was great! My school teacher assigned us a piece of literature to read in class, but since most of the class wasn't finished by the time the period was over, she told us to go home and search for 'To Build A Fire' by Jack London online. I went to Google Books and found a perfect version of the short story. I would recommend Google Books and eBooks to other people."

SENIOR POETRY

Second Place

Rose Condon
North Carolina, USA

Prayer

Oh, God, I'd like a moon
To light the path I tread –
My hope is wearing thin,
My heart is full of dread.
You said that night will end:
Well, it can't end too soon,
And on that subject, God,
I'd really like a moon.

Oh, God, please send a star,
To guide me home tonight,
Like you did long ago
To give the Wise Men light.
This trail is awfully dark
And twists and turns afar,
So if it's fine with You,
I wouldn't mind a star.

Oh, God, just give a light,
To keep me on the way,
There's roots and stones and holes
And it's nine hours till day –
I know that You are here,
But it's so dark tonight,
So if You would, dear God,
Please shine me down some light.

Biography:
When not doing schoolwork, Rose is nearly always seen with her nose in a book, or else working on her cherry-red laptop computer. She also loves music, especially singing, and belongs to a youth choir. She avoids sports, but likes outdoor activities like hiking, tree-climbing, archery, and boating. She loves dogs and cats equally, but draws the line at snakes. Her favorite season is autumn.

Commentary on eBooks:
"I have not had much experience with eBooks, but I'd like to learn more. I think that since people do so much with computers nowadays, it's only a matter of time until they read books on them."

Third Place

Leon Li
Maryland, USA

So Long As I Breathe

Until it takes our lives, there is little to fear.
We still see its type every day of the year.
This other type of dying takes neither me nor you,
But severs our lives, dividing zero by two.
For we live in one another - you are my validation -
When we die in each other, how is the separation
Any different from death when I die by myself?
It's identical except you're departing as well.
No man's an island, but we all know the sea
With waves that turn violent so easily,
That leaves silence unbridged, which I struggle to cross
Where your music lived, and now, my one-sided
       thoughts.
Though the storms change our paths, wherever I go
With me I'll always have your aliveness, your soul.
So as long as I breathe, never will I say
'You are dead to me,' lest I die too that day.

Biography:
Leon receives his poetic inspiration in the woods near his house. He envisions himself as a traveling poet but due to the oppressive conditions of the world on human passions, he has chosen to pursue business for a career. Every day he feels grateful to his friends.

Commentary on eBooks:
"I publish my poems on my blog, and my friends do too. We read each others' blogs."

Award of Excellence

Emily Forberg
Illinois, USA

Nightly Routine

Gently remove our daytime skins.
Our fabrics, itching us, scratching us.
Making us uncomfortable.
Take them off. Into the hamper they go.
It's not enough.
Itches. Scratches. They persist.
More. More. Closer to birth than we've been since
that fatefulfateful day.
Come clean. Cleaner than ever before.
Down to skin and bones.
Our bare bodies.
Knobby knees. Rigid ribs. Hard hips.
Milky white skin. Pearlescent in the moonglow.
Tonight's darkness trapping our flesh.
Peel away the layers. The skin is too much.
Loosen it up. Slide the meat off our bones.
Tendons, muscles relax. Create slack, then pull back.
String by string. Gone. Everything.
The blood trickles to the floor.
Making a mess, but keeping us clean. Cleansed.
Free. Our bones hollow stone.
Our skeletons clanking, clashing.
Becoming brittle. We snap. Crack.
The scrapes and flakes amount.
The bones shaking and falling.
Together. 'Til we're all just
one big pile of dust.

Just waiting for the morning cleaning crew to come
sweep us up.

~~~~

Biography:
Emily Forberg is a senior in high school, and loves every
second of it. She is very involved, especially in the
drama department, appearing onstage in the fall plays
and improv, and also competing on the speech team.
After high school, Emily plans on taking a gap year to
travel the world. She then plans on going to college to
major in theatre.

Commentary on eBooks:
"Regarding eBooks and ePublishing, I don't know much,
but it seems like a sound concept. What with the Kindle
and other types of electronics starting to replace the
traditional book, online availability of literature seems
like a good idea. What I'm wondering, though is how
will the issue of illegal downloads be handled? When
music became available online, immediately sites where
one could download music for free cut into the profits of
both the musicians and legal sites. What can be done to
make sure the same doesn't happen to authors and eBook
websites?"

Honorable Mention

Nurul Haya
Maryland, USA

Presbyopia

There were cracks on her skin.

He palmed her softly,
afraid to breach
the aged carapace.

It's been years,
he whispered,
her side deflating
like a collapsed lung.

She became old;
rough,
cumbersome.

So he left her
not knowing that inside,
her flesh was still
green.

Biography:
Nurul does not claim to be an artist, only an admirer of beautiful things (such as books). She hopes her efforts at writing will be beautiful to someone.

Commentary on eBooks:
"I own an eReader, so I appreciate the convenience of eBooks. eBooks are more environmentally sound and perhaps more appealing aesthetically - the polished surfaces of their containers mimic those of video game systems - yet one cannot forsake the lovely aged leafs of a true book. I am fond of my little reading machine, but I also love the smell and feel of old books. I hope they will not become extinct."

Judges' Award

Nicholas Turton
New York, USA

One Thousand Thoughts

One thousand thoughts pushing and pressing,
On the one mind choked by monumental stress.
Our slaving lives becoming labored and meaningless,
As we are rushed into respiratory arrest.

But do we ever pause, and stop?

And listen to our tired breath?
Or inhale the exuberant scene of life?
Or taste the pure, fresh air for what it truly is?

No, we never let ourselves breathe deeply,
Unable to gaze at the breathless scene around,
Always holding the breath within…

Now,
Breathe the world and our souls anew with
A thousand deep breaths,
Forgetting the thousand thoughts before.

Biography:
Nicholas Turton is highly intelligent, easy going, and friendly. Growing up in a small town, he wishes to attend college in a big city. He is working his way to become a freelance artist majoring in graphic design. He dreams of designing album covers for popular bands, movie posters for films on the silver screen, and setting trends by designing T-shirts.

Commentary on eBooks:
"eBooks seem like a cool way to transport books and media. I think they are a good step in the right direction in the form of literature and media. I don't really know a lot about eBooks, but from what I've seen, they seem very interesting."

SENIOR SHORT STORIES

First Place

Laura Hoelzl
New York, USA

Salt

"Do you want fries with that?"

I glance over at you, questioning. Meeting my eyes, you hesitate for a moment, then grin.

"Yes, please."

"Supersize?"

Again I consult your face for the answer. Your grin grows wider in response, spreading to your clear blue eyes.

"Absolutely."

The cashier disinterestedly punches buttons on the register. I hand over a wad of crumpled bills, but my mind is suddenly elsewhere. In these last few moments, a floodgate had been opened. Anyone else at this unremarkable highway rest stop would have no idea, but the two of us understand perfectly.

I collect the tray covered in grease-stained paper, noting the flat foil patties slapped on gaudy logos. In the center glows the chest of gold— fried fingers of potato glittering with salt. The sight of them, their tantalizing smell, the thought of the imminent consumption... It's absolutely overwhelming. I place the plastic tray on a corner table with a design patterned to disguise crumbs and we count our remaining funds. We then advance from counter to counter, like a pair of lionesses systematically stalking a line of tasty zebras. We order with reckless abandon, barely checking price or product.

"What is that?"

"I have no idea, but it looks delicious."

"We'll take two, please."

Finally we are down to pennies. You balance two trays piled with an ungodly amount of food. Wrappers perch haphazardly in some sort of bizarre edible sculpture. Paper and plastic mix with assorted confections of sugar and grease, fruit in various stages of preservation, salty crisps in every form imaginable, and one restaurant's entire value menu. I hold another tray heaped equally ridiculously and balance four Pepsis and two yogurt parfaits in my left arm. We manage to stop at the condiment station, squirting ketchup and mustard and relish where they are needed. The fries are waiting as we shuffle back to the table, careful not to upset the mountains upon our trays.

Seated on metal-backed chairs bolted to the sticky floor, we behold the magnificent display spread before us. You pull out your phone to digitally document the experience. We stare in silent awe for several moments, then—at an unspoken signal—we peel back the first of the wrappers and the gorging commences. I proceed from one foil-encased delicacy to the next, only beginning another once the previous has disappeared. You sample everything at once, grabbing mouthfuls from three worldwide chains at once.

To the strangers glancing at us from the corners of their eyes, we look like two average teenage girls enjoying our high metabolism. One rather rotund woman's glare sizes up this week's worth of calories assembled before us. She assumes we take our gorging abilities for granted. We obviously believe that we'll stay a size 0 forever, but she knows one day these calories will sink directly to our bloated thighs.

She has no idea that a year ago you were a skeleton. She has no idea that these are your first French fries in twelve months, twelve months that took years off your life and almost ended it. For it was 365 days ago that you cut out all kinds of food like this spread across the table. You sought perfection and when you could not achieve it through restriction, you resorted to elimination.

The rest of us watched the whole degeneration, something we'll never forgive ourselves for. We pleaded, we screamed, we cried. We tried force; we tried sympathy. Intervention failed yet letting you learn the hard way would have soon killed you. The symptoms need not be listed; they may be found in any textbook. The causes, however, were more personal than I can put into words. You were absolutely determined for all the wrong reasons. You deteriorated on the outside after you had ravaged yourself on the inside.

Then you hit rock bottom. Smashed, crashed, splintered into a million defeated pieces. It was a while before you could rise back up, literally, out of your hospital bed. It was even longer before you could walk, and nearly an eternity before you could run again. Now we're returning from a major track meet where you ran your best time ever.

To this day, I cannot fathom from what depths you drew your strength. Perhaps it was pure survival instinct, the superhuman strength that arises in a moment of need. That day you stood in front of the mirror and screamed and screamed and couldn't stop... Look at you now. The scars are not immediately apparent to the inexperienced eye, but we both know they will never disappear entirely. For now, you're whole again, and it's not just skin deep. Looking at you, I see life. I feel life, both yours and mine.

Suddenly the back of my throat is burning and my chicken nuggets are impossible to swallow. My vision blurs and I squeeze my eyelids shut, trying to quell the scalding wave rising behind them. A year ago I was convinced I had lost you, and I had mourned. Folding printed foil, I struggle to maintain a steady measure of breathing through my closing throat. This is no place to break down. Breathe.

The wrappers are empty now, mere shells of foil like caloric carcasses strewn about a greasy plain. All that remains are the French fries. We each select one: a fat floppy one for you, a skinny crispy one for me. We dip them in ketchup and pause. We look at each other, sharing emotions too deep for words. The wave breaks through my lids and a prick of fire slides down my cheek, dropping onto the fry. I place it in my mouth. The salt burns.

"Good fries."

~~~~

Biography:
Laura Hoelzl is a creative person who expresses herself through pencils and sneakers. She enjoys reading and writing, and is an avid runner. She hopes to one day see her work recognized, but not her name.

Commentary on eBooks:
"I have never personally used an eBook, but I find the idea fascinating. Combining what appear to be two incompatible fields, English and technology, ePublishing makes reading more convenient in a world where size and speed are vital. The gadget fiend is able to appreciate literature like never before."

Second Place

Ioana Grosu
Michigan, USA

Wake Up Call

It was with tear-filled eyes that I bade farewell to my brother. It is a hard thing, to see someone that you care for, and to know that they only have a short amount of time before they depart this world. I did not understand why he had to do that- to die so suddenly. All my life, I had considered him a hero, someone to look up to. He was brave and strong. He helped me through challenging schoolwork. He never let me down when it felt like the world was against me. Even though I was younger, he did not look at me as his inferior—rather, as more of a student, and I admired him even more.

When he finally left to go and carry out his mission, I was sitting in the main room of our small apartment. A monotone ticking from the clock on the wall was the only noise in the room. I held my breath, imagining my brother in his last moments. Was he scared? Probably not. When he left, he was in a crazed, almost ecstatic state. He kept grinning, and occasionally laughed lightheartedly.

It frightened me, how willing he was to give his life away. For years, he had been training for this one moment- "to make a difference," he used to tell me. In my mind, I was proud, but in my soul, I knew that it was wrong. What difference would it make if he killed some soldiers? Or worse, some civilians? I felt terrible for questioning his cause, but as the minutes were slowly drained away, I resented those who were forcing him into this.

I looked up at the awful object on the wall. It seemed to oppress me, with its unceasing noise. A few more minutes passed, and I feared that I would go insane. My heart was pounding and my head was spinning. I felt like vomiting from the anxiety.

Then, the dreaded hour came. I could almost feel the explosion shake me, and my spirit shattering with my brother's body. The militants who trained him were probably jubilant-- more of their enemies were killed. But I...I just felt cold, empty, as if the life was sucked out of me, and I was left with an empty shell.

Was I a bad person, for not agreeing with their ideas? For doubting the fact that this senseless violence could bring about anything good?

Unable to stand the heat and the heavy atmosphere in the room, I stood up, and walked outside. Soldiers were stationed along the sides of the roads, and they smiled at me as I passed. I ignored them, averting my gaze downwards. Were they bad people? They were always kind to me, even though I was an unimportant little girl. But they were the enemy, the reason my brother died.

A tiny cloud of dust arose from under my feet as I shuffled forward, closer to the spot that my brother was sent to. I could hear shouts, and a muffled sob. Stepping closer, I saw the charred side of a building, and a fire, which people were desperately trying to put out. I did not want to see any more. I did not want to face the truth.

Despite what I had been taught, I could not force myself to believe that what he did was good. Even if it caused me to hate myself, I did not want to end up like him. He was not a hero. He was a murderer. I did not want to hate him, but I could not praise him either.

Both my mind and my soul came to that one conclusion, and I could deny it no longer. I vowed that I would help change things. I would make a difference, but not in the way that my brother attempted. His memory saddened me, but his death taught me something. I wanted to be good, but in my sense of the word.

That time, when I walked to my apartment, I smiled back at the soldiers.

~~~~

Biography:
Ioana Grosu loves to eat sushi while thinking of new ideas for her writing. Her hobbies include: procrastinating, taking walks outside, and martial arts. She hopes to study philosophy later on.

Commentary on eBooks:
I think that eBooks and ePublishing are great ways to get works across to the rest of the world. They would save money on paper and binding, and would be easy to access for many people. Although, I would prefer it if there is a printed version as well, because it is more tangible, and has more value.

Third Place

Darrah Moul
Michigan, USA

True Royalty

I was at my friend Felicia's house for a sleepover when the doorbell rang. Not wanting to miss any fun, I sprinted to open the door. But my laughter from the movie playing the living room died abruptly as I saw my mom stood there, with tears sliding down her face.

"Emmaline." She choked. "We're going to Grandma's house. There...There was a fire. Our house is gone," and she broke off as the tears threatened to overcome her.

I stared at her, certain that I had heard wrong. Then slowly it sank in. Our house was *gone*. My world tipped and my head began to pound. After dizzily stuffing my overnight bag into the trunk, I climbed into the car and we drove into the snowy night.

After a few more minutes, Mom turned off the road and pulled into the driveway. The lights on Grandma's porch taunted my numb brain with their cheeriness. Grandma opened the door before Mom could ring the doorbell and stood there, her arms open wide. She was wearing the soft, yellow cashmere sweater that Mom had bought her for Christmas last year. She hugged us and led us to the living room where my dad, brother, and sister were sitting in an awkward silence. I hugged dad, then, tired and unsure, joined him and my younger sister, Lily, on the couch. Lily turned and gave me a great big hug, as if to say, "Everything will be okay. You'll see."

Grandma tried to tempt us with fresh cookies, but looking around at my family now sitting in silence in a living room not our own, I knew things would never be the same.

About an hour later, I nestled in a sleeping bag on the floor in Grandma's living room. I needed to sleep, but I was all but relaxed. I had a million questions: *How did the fire happen? Where were we going to live? Did we have enough money for a new house?* I knew I should just be thankful we were all safe, but the materialistic part of me couldn't stop thinking about all the things that were lost: everything from Mom's good china, to all of Dad's files that he needed to teach Biology at the university, to my brother Ethan's expensive stereo, right down to my lava lamp.

I should've known that we wouldn't stay at Grandma's for long. The next morning Dad woke me and told me we were leaving after breakfast. It took a minute for my brain to wake up and remember. My first thought was that only a pile of ashes remained of the room where I had spent probably half my life, and that sent a shiver down my spine.

"Where are we going?" I asked, groggily.

"Your mother found us a hotel." Dad replied.

"Why don't we stay with Grandma?" I would normally love to stay at a hotel, but the fact that I didn't have my swimsuit and everyone there would see how poor we now were made me long for Grandma's cashmere and cookies instead.

"Because we don't want to make her feel like we're her responsibility," he said.

I pushed myself up and followed him to the kitchen.

Everyone else was already gathered around the table, with a rainbow of breakfast foods spread out before them. I quickly took the only empty chair at the table and glanced around.

Grandma smiled at me warmly, and Mom said good morning. Ethan looked annoyed, but Lily just ate. I decided to go with Lily's outlook.

Breakfast was silent – any attempt at conversation was smothered by the fear that buttered our toast.

We finished breakfast and hugged Grandma goodbye, then got into the car. We rode in silence, and a couple of minutes later pulled into a motel parking lot. Dad parked the car, and we all got out.

Lily wore her princess crown on her head - she was rarely seen without some sort of princess attire. Dad led the way, but Lily really led us all. She skipped up next to him, her snow boots clunking, tiara atop her head, and held his hand. She wasn't afraid of what anyone else thought, and I envied her for that. But she seemed to lift our spirits, for we all walked into the hotel lobby, to the elevator, and into our room with our heads held high.

Lily ran through the room and flopped down on the bed. "That went well," she said with a satisfied sigh. We all looked at her in a puzzled silence. "I was half afraid someone was going to start crying when the guy at the desk asked how long we would be staying. Or when he told us that the pool was down the hall and to the right," Lily said, pausing to take a breath. When she saw that we still didn't understand what she was trying to say, she continued. "Seeing as we don't have swimming suits to swim in," she informed us. "The pool is of no use to us." Her important-sounding tone made us all smile. Then Dad got a funny twinkle in his eye. The corners of his mouth twitched. Lily noticed, and sat up straighter, adjusting the crown on top of her head. She raised her eyebrows, smiled at Dad disapprovingly, and said in her royal tone, "Sire, princesses *do not* go skinny dipping."

Every single one of us burst out laughing. Maybe it was the scratched, painted tiara that sat atop a flame of tangled red-orange hair. Or maybe it was the tone of her voice that almost convinced us she *was* a princess. Whatever it was, as we doubled over with laughter, I suddenly realized: I don't need a house to be happy. I don't even need to know where I will spend the next night or where I will get my next meal. No, all I need is my family. Because when I am with them, I am royalty.

~~~~

Biography:
Darrah Moul is a freshman in high school and enjoys playing piano and flute and being in the marching band. She loves chocolate, friends, family, and her puppy, Tessa. Darrah also likes writing, but does not like cleaning the house. Her big dream for the future is to get a degree in music and minor in interior design.

Commentary on eBooks:
"I know that eBooks are an electronic way to publish something. They can be bought and read on a computer or other device. I am currently saving for an eBook reader so that I can own and carry many books at once. And I think it is cool technology."

Award of Excellence

Jessica Lumanta
Hawaii, USA

Bal Masque: The Masquerade Ball

A bright full moon lit up France's sky on the night of the ball. Hundreds of gentry gathered together on the momentous evening. All were clad in extravagantly vivid attire, their mischievous eyes peering out from behind regal masks. The air was thick with shrill laughter, the putrid odor of liquor, and bright flashes of colors exploded in the sky. The sea of people went on endlessly.

The main square at the foot of the palace buzzed with excitement. Musicians lightened the mood with merry songs as the masked guests danced jollily and ate their fill of the feast that was set out by the King. Foreign circus performers dazzled the crowds with their antics as colorful floats were carried around in a parade. Like a jewel in a crown, the Royal Family sat in the middle of the festival.

"Damien," the King whispered to the Crown Prince, "Why are you not bearing the sword that I gave you?"

The Prince shifted uneasily and sighed. "I'm sorry, Father, but while my men and I were out hunting the day after you gave me the sword, a thief attacked us in the woods and stole all our valuable possessions. Please forgive my carelessness."

The King sighed and rubbed his forehead. "Those selfish, money-hungry thieves should all be beheaded. Don't worry, son. We will catch that thief and bring him to justice."

"He was quite unusual, Father," the Prince said. "I didn't get to see his face, but I did notice that he wore a

84

silver locket."

The King laughed. "A locket? What an unusual thief indeed."

"Oh, Annette!" the Queen suddenly cried. "Stop playing with that necklace. I told you that those sapphires are a priceless family heirloom."

"Please, stop nagging, Mother," the crude Princess howled. "It's almost time for the dance."

A figure appeared amidst the crowd with clothes darker than a raven's feathers, a simple black hat, and an ornate mask. The sound of the figure's leather boots hitting the pavement was muffled by the commotion of the Masquerade.

The figure boldly approached the Crown Princess's throne and extended a gloved hand. "May I have this dance, Princess?"

The Princess's cheeks flushed as she gave a crooked smile, and her tall, pirate ship headdress quivered. She accepted the invitation and strutted onto the dance floor. The Princess and the mysterious figure danced smoothly. The Princess turned and dipped elegantly as if she didn't have two left feet.

"Oh! This has been absolutely splendid," she cooed nasally. "May I have the pleasure of knowing your name, Monsieur?"

The mysterious figure remained unmoved like the moon in the sky. "You needn't know my name, Princess."

With a tip of the hat, the figure ran off and disappeared. The Princess sighed dreamily. As she put her hands over her chest, she gasped and looked down at her bare neck.

"Thief!" she cried. "That man stole my jewels!"

The Masquerade went into a frenzy as the dark figure tore through the performers. Within minutes, the guards took off through the crowd with the Prince in the lead.

The masked thief swept through the crowds with ease and clambered up onto the decorative floats. The Prince and the guards did the same. The men chased the thief over the floats twenty feet above the crowd. Once the thief was within reach, the prince leaped into the air, swinging his sword toward the masked thief.

Just as the two swords collided, the Prince noticed a silver locket dangling from the thief's neck. "You!"

The prince swung his sword again, and it came down swiftly, slapping the hat away and chopping off half of the thief's mask. The hat hit the dusty pavement gently while the mask shattered to pieces.

Long, wavy brown hair cascaded down the thief's back, and an elegant nose and a pair of thin red lips were uncovered.

"It is a woman!" a man in the crowd cried.

In the blink of an eye, the commotion caused the two gigantic floats to collide, making them rattle violently. The Prince could no longer hold his balance, and he tumbled off the float. Completely helpless, he shut his eyes, preparing himself for an excruciating pain.

However, his eyes snapped open when he felt a tug at his wrist. The crowd gasped in awe as the prince dangled in the air, saved by the thief herself. The thief's deep brown eyes peered out from behind the remains of the mask, not with the cold stare of a thief, but something completely different. She grunted and roughly pulled the Prince back onto the float.

"Wait!" the Prince cried as she turned to run. "Who are you?"

The thief remained silent, her thin red lips twisted into a smirk.

She pounced gracefully off the float, grabbing the end of one of the hanging banners and swung over the Masquerade. The crowd gasped in awe as she soared over their heads. She swooped down, snatched her hat, and landed at the end of a dark alley.

Before she left, she turned back and tipped her hat. "Au revoir."

With that, she disappeared from sight.

"What in blazes is going on here?" the King shouted furiously, running up to the Prince's side.

The Prince remained bewildered, recollecting himself and remembering the mysterious masked thief. "I think that thief just saved my life."

Bella de Ruél crouched on the roof of a tall building, looking back over at the commotion at the Palace. She reached into her pocket and revealed the sparkling gems. She smiled and clutched her mother's silver locket against her chest as she thought of what that single sapphire necklace would mean to the poor, goodhearted people in her village. As she smiled, the deep blue of the sapphires sparkled in the moonlight and reflected in her eyes. With one final glance at the Masquerade Ball, Bella de Ruél turned and disappeared amongst the shadows of France.

~~~~

Biography:
Besides reading and writing, Jessica enjoys eating, drawing, playing the piano, guitar, and ukulele, spending time with family, and listening to music, including SHINee and Super Junior. Her goal is to improve in her writing skills and to publish a book in the near future.

Commentary on eBooks:
I do know about eBooks. However, I prefer to read the old-fashioned way.

Honorable Mention

Brittaney Leeper
Massachusetts, USA

Ready or Not

Kika didn't flinch as the rusty door of her cage opened with a loud screech. She'd been in this rust pot for long enough to get used to it. The sight of her overseer, however, was a completely different story.

It was hard not to notice the six-foot-six-inch tall giant, who made even Kika feel short, entering through the three-foot-thick steel doors. As usual, he seemed to enjoy the discomfort of everyone around him, especially Kika. Scars covered his body, some of which Kika had given him, which had caused quite a few "punishments." These punishments took a major toll on Kika's body, especially in her weakened state. Of course, his huge muscles mixed with his short temper didn't help her physical state at all.

He seemed a little off to Kika, edgy in a way. He began to pace her cage, glancing at her in disgust. Kika simply glared at him from her tiny cot, trying to not move a muscle, in fear of a shock from her oh-so-lovely collar. Fifty laps around her cage later, he stopped to sneer at her, causing Kika to snarl as best she could.

"Turns out that the *ikele* has ignored my wishes to let you rot here and wants to use you out in the field again," he growled, sounding almost like a bear. "Yet another one is loose, and people are beginning to grow suspicious of the signs it has left. You are to track it down and stop it...*quickly*."

Kika cocked her head as the word quickly implied something that she hated to do. This was to be one of her rare kill missions. That would be hard for her to choose to do, let alone manage. She considered trying to bargain or to simply say no, but then her collar gave her a "reminder" of what she was at the moment. A slave.

"Can I at least have something to eat first? Or are you going to try and starve me as you originally planned?" Kika asked, putting as much hatred and sarcasm into her voice as she could.

He scowled right before pressing a hand held button, causing her to wince as a shock went through her body.

Stupid wireless buttons.

"Come now, or else we might have to find another to train," he growled. "After all, it seems your kind are easily domesticated."

Kika struggled with the urge to attack him. Injuring him might just cause a huge shock to be given, and most likely her ending up bruised and battered. *Again.* She forced herself to lower her head and rise slowly to her feet.

"Fine let's go. I needed to go outside and stretch my legs out anyway," Kika said, sniffing almost daintily in disgust. The overseer snorted in disappointment before moving behind Kika, prepared to shock her if she "misbehaved." The doors swung open in their slow way, revealing a large van, with its back hatch open.

Damn, Kika thought. *This must be serious. The ikele has never needed me to get to a drop-off so quickly.*

Kika started to walk towards the van, with the overseer walking directly behind her, shoving her whenever she was too slow for his tastes...which was often. Kika felt the childish urge to rip his throat out, but she knew better. Plus, she would be punished for such an act of violence. It was against the rules. *Stupid people and their silly rules.*

Kika felt relief as she walked into the van; the overseer wasn't allowed in the transport, which meant she could mentally prepare for the fight to come. The door shut as she settled into the padded seats, closing her eyes to rest.

The engine's hum grew into a full-out growl, and the van began to race along the roads, trying to reach the drop-off zone ASAP. Kika snoozed, waiting for her time to move freely again.

A light screech woke Kika from her nap; the van had stopped. Kika quickly moved to the hatch, waiting for it to open. A slight hiss rose from the hinges when the hatch opened, causing Kika to shift her weight in impatience. As soon as it was wide enough to slip though, she left the small cage-like room to reach the night and the forest.

Kika smiled as the scent of the forest reached her nose; it had been too long since she had been out of the metal cage. A laugh almost came from her mouth when Kika suddenly remembered why she had come back to the forest in the first place. *To kill.* She stopped smiling and began to search the dark forest for a clearing where the moon beams shone. It didn't take long; the drivers of the van had parked near one.

Kika took a deep breath before entering the clearing. At first nothing happened. *Like always.* But then the magic started. She grew in size, her now black fur growing in huge tufts, while her body began to take the wolf appearance she enjoyed so much. Her fangs and claws glinted in the now bright light of the moon. The shadows flickered wildly, magic flowing though the air in huge amounts. Kika continued to grow until she was nearly ten feet tall.

Her body was still covered in the scars of battles won and lost in the past. The body of one of the strongest form of werewolves...*an alpha*. Stronger still, since her mate had died, killed by the humans.

At the end, Kika felt the freedom that this form

caused and the unusual aggression. A scent of another werewolf caught her complete attention. It was a full grown male, not an alpha. Most importantly, it was in Kika's territory. She narrowed her golden eyes and took in large breaths, trying to trace where the scent came from.

A howl caused her to grin. The male was probably trying to attract a mate. He had just given her the basic direction he was in. Kika bounded towards the direction of the male's howl, her fur making her look like yet another shadow of the night.

Ready or not. Here I come, Kika thought as she raced toward the intruder.

~~~~

Biography:
Brittaney wants to become a small animal veterinarian. She lives with her parents, her younger brother, and younger sister....and their zoo of pets, including three dogs, five cats (and some kits), and her two geckos. She likes reading, writing, drawing, and listening to music while drawing or writing. She won Honorable Mention in Middle School Poetry, with "Her Pups" in the 2009 New Voices Young Writers Competition.

Commentary on eBooks:
"My mother bought me an eBookwise reader a few years back, and it makes life a little simpler. Carrying one electronic reader with multiple books in it sure beats carrying five or six large books. Though charging it gets annoying at some points."

Judges' Award

Clare Nowak
Colorado, USA

Wind Chimes

Jason's feet made him stumble as he trudged through the dreary, darkening streets. His feet felt like cinder blocks, and his tennis shoes were sopping wet as his lazy pace took him through muddy puddles. His socks were serving to steal all heat from his lower body, since they were soaking wet and cold too. There was a steady breeze blowing down the small alley, and the sky was so thick with gray rain clouds, he wouldn't have known it was dawn. For all he cared, he had been walking at least a few months.

Shouldn't have checked the mail yesterday, he rebuked himself. The elegant lettering and ivory envelope should have told him not to pick it up. He'd picked it out from the bills and junk he usually received in his dump of an apartment. He should have expected something nasty when he'd seen the "to Mister Rushing" on the front, and no one *ever* called him that.

He hardly lifted his eyes as the first stubborn raindrops fell from the clouds, hands deep in his pockets. It didn't take long for the stubborn drizzle to break into a fully functioning rainstorm. He was too caught up in his thoughts to notice the rain or that he had turned out of the alley onto the main road. He was resolute to ignore the rain, although it was plastering his clothes to his skin, his hair to his head and causing that burning in the back of his sore throat to worsen. He coughed in such a manner that the back of his swollen throat seemed to suffer a blow with a meat tenderizer. His nose lost feeling and his ears were beginning to ache. With a muttered curse, he took shelter inside a quaint little antique shop.

Of course the envelope wasn't the part that had him in this half-human state. What was inside the envelope had been far worse. "Cordially invited," the white invitation had read. "Katherine and Matthew cordially invite you to their wedding." What irony it was, that Matthew, the lout who could hardly tell his right from his left would marry Kate, who, even when she was a little girl, had been the head of every class she'd ever been in.

Jason turned to look out the windows of the dusty, dirty shop. He rubbed his ears with numb hands in an attempt to get rid of the headache his frozen ears had caused him. A little old lady in an ugly flower print dress was smiling at him from behind the counter, hoping he'd decide to buy one of her useless oddities scattered about the shop. She must not have noticed he was nearly soaked to the bone, as all she did was jut her head out like a goose and smile. Jason scarcely acknowledged the woman's existence as he examined the dull shop.

A broken grandfather clock the old woman had set up in the far corner of the store stood tall and tilted. Isolated from all the other clocks, which had been set up in the window, it stood, waiting to fall apart piece by piece. No one was going to buy that thing; it was cheap, but it was ugly and useless. The chipped glass plate over the face of the clock, the twisted hands, its tall stature that made it look sinister—it wasn't something any sweet, intelligent girl would want to keep around.

Whether he'd get hypothermia in going out or not, Jason could stand the dinky antique store no longer. He trudged for the door, when a sudden spark of light in his eye made him stop. Turning at the sudden flash, his eyes caught hold of a spinning piece of cut glass hanging on a string, turning and twisting slowly. Despite himself, he walked towards it.

It looked to be the end of a wind chime, and the fake gem sat dangling with other smaller pieces of cut glass like it. It took a moment for Jason's memory to bring back the picture of his childhood which had little to do with that particular wind chime, but he was certain it was the very same that had hung in Kate's room of the apartment building they had both grown up in. How it had ended up in an antique shop he didn't know. Lazy afternoons and faded summer days that had long since been filed away in his mind were opened and dusted off so he might look at them, like old photographs, again. He and Kate had grown up together. They were, according to her, "practically family."

"You have to be there," she had said. "Who else is going to walk me down the aisle?" That was the way it was done. Send him on a guilt trip to make him come to the wedding. She knew how to get what she wanted from him, and, despite himself, Jason smiled grimly for a moment. At least there was one thing her leech of a fiancé hadn't managed to take away from her.

Matthew, that was the rich boy's name. Matthew, the guy who wouldn't know a day's work if it ran him over on the freeway; the man who went for annual facials and perms; the man who was marrying Kate in two weeks just because he got lucky.

Jason's hand cupped around one of the winding gems. It was cool and smooth, perfectly clear…like the diamond that sat in Kate's ring and almost as big.

As for Jason, he would be the one filling in for Kate's father—giving her away in more ways than anyone would care to know. He wasn't the type to leap up in the middle of the preacher's reading with an "I object." He wasn't the type to rush in at the last moment in hopes of sweeping the princess off her feet. He wasn't a prince. He was the guy watching Cinderella leave the ball with the Prince who'd found her slipper.

With a final farewell to the wind chime, dangling and glittering in the window, Jason turned out of the store and into the rain, lost in faded pictures of summers past.

~~~~

Biography:
Clare began writing stories when she was about six. She enjoys reading classical literature, writing (she's written two novels and is working on a third), hiking, acting, hanging out with her friends and family. Writing and music are her passions. She listens to every kind of music from Mozart, Yiruma, and the Vitamin String Quartet to Eve 6, the Killers and the All-American Rejects. Her favorite and best subject in school is English, which she plans to major in when she graduates high school.

Commentary on eBooks:
'I love surfing the Internet. It's so easy to find information -- it's like having every library in the world at your fingertips. I'm not very educated on eBooks specifically, but I am interested to learn. Though I'm not sure at all on the specifics regarding ePublishing, I think the idea sounds very interesting and I'm keen to learn more about it.'

SENIOR ESSAYS

First Place

Katie Guyot
Kansas, USA

On Dorkiness

In a world where fashion is redefined every season and gas prices rise and fall with the sun, any form of stability is generally a comfort. Such is the case with the cheery rainbow of insults and nicknames available in the English language, which can almost always be found extending all the way from the kindergarten playground to the broad, square roof of the public high school.

I do not mean to imply that today's citizens stage verbal attacks in Shakespeare's tongue ("thou frothy, elf-skinned dewberry" is not a phrase commonly heard on the subway), but instead that very few changes have been made in this particular area of modern slang over the past decade. It is a consolation of sorts to know that I have belonged to the same social category since elementary school, and that I will probably continue to be categorized similarly until graduation. It is because of this deceptive sense of security that I nearly choked to death on oxygen when, while using my spare time in Beginning Journalism to flip through a nearby dictionary rather than chat with my classmates, I stumbled upon the word "dork."

This is a noun that I have grown quite fond of over the years; a noun that graces my lips nine out of every ten times that I am asked to describe myself. I always assumed that it was synonymous with my name: one who has brains rather than brawn, is pathetically obsessed with grammar and sentence fluency, would rather stay home reading Agatha Christie novels than venture into a school dance, and spends her summers surfing college websites and studying for the SATs. As it so happens, I was painfully wrong.

My most primitive identity had betrayed me, for between "Doric" and "dorm" laid the description of an introverted, awkward recluse who lacks basic intelligence. Thanks to this monumental stab in the back, I am now forced to reconsider my very being as I am faced with the difficult task of choosing a replacement for my beloved expression of self-deprecation.

Like the [insert noun to illustrate my previous, incorrect definition of "dork" here] I am, I decided to get a second opinion before fully accepting my mistake, so I thrust my arms elbow-deep into the all-knowing Internet and consulted the experts.

First to step up to the podium was *Dictionary.com*, which envisions a dork as a dim-witted, bizarre, possibly mean version of a nerd. Contrarily, its two definitions of "nerd" portray either a phenomenally smart or phenomenally stupid person, and because the two cancel each other out, not much knowledge can be gained there. Personally, I have only ever heard the word used in reference to the former, but then, my intuition has already been proved futile by more than one website. For instance, *The Free Dictionary*'s dork is an incompetent idiot and *Wikipedia*'s a strange, inelegant buffoon. My confidence level may not be well up to par, but I do not actually view myself as this much of an oddball.

While I cannot argue that I possess great social poise, seeing as how this entire expedition began while reading a dictionary to avoid having to hold a conversation with a cheerleader, I sincerely hope that *Urban Dictionary*'s member Danny Moules has not accurately described me in his explanation: "Dork is a derogatory term for someone with few social skills, usually interested in nerdy activities and immediately makes a poor impression through their lack of social aptitude."

I am almost certain that there is currently an arrow engraved with dear Danny's name sticking out of my bleeding self-esteem. Thank you, Urban Dictionary, for effectively dashing any hopes I may have had for becoming anything but a hermit after my senior year.

Now that I have been enlightened with the truth about dorks, I realize that certain insults that have been aimed at me in the past are even more insulting than I once gave them credit for. When I was in seventh grade (my junior high, an American oddity, contained grades seven through nine), an athletic, academically gifted, attractive, and altogether aggravating freshman approached me after gym class to comment on my neatly ironed sweater vest.

"The dorky style is very in right now," he managed over stifled laughter. As he walked away into the wave of undisguised chortling echoing about his lackeys' corner, he added, "It suits you."

Why thank you, I thought. That's exactly what I needed to boost my confidence.

Of course I grasped the belittling nature of his "compliment," but at the time, my comprehension was, apparently, limited. In fact, most of my experience with the subject stemmed from the popular nickname dubbed upon players of stringed instruments (such as myself, a violist): "Orch Dork." Our retaliation was naturally the phrase, "Band geek," which we thought evened out the offense. After all, did the two words not mean the same thing? We believed this to be a rhetorical question, but my recent research proves otherwise.

While "geek" can be substituted for "inelegant but scholarly computer prodigy," "dork" is merely a replacement for "maladroit and dense social outcast." Embarrassing as it is to admit an entire guild's mistake, I am slightly soothed to learn that I am not the only person confused by slang's ever-changing scope.

Because language is always transforming, it is completely possible that the definition of dork will be utterly altered in a few years' time. Already, its connotations have been distorted to enrapture Dungeons & Dragons fanatics and bookworms alike.

By the time I rename myself something less self-devaluing, "dork" will have taken on an entirely new meaning, and all of my careful planning will be for naught. Perhaps, then, I should continue to refer to myself as a dork and pretend to be none the wiser. After all, only someone who has spent a considerable amount of time investigating modern slang would catch my mistake, and only a true dork would do something that preposterous.

~~~~

Biography:
Katie is a high school sophomore with a long-running addiction to literature. Though she loves to read and write above all else, the vast majority of her time is spent studying and chopping away at a looming mountain of homework assignments. Tedious as her workload can seem, she hopes that it will aid her in accomplishing her dream to become an editor and a novelist.

Commentary on eBooks:
"I personally have never used an eBook, but it seems that I am one of the few who can say this honestly. I know many people who swear by online material, whether reading for pleasure or otherwise, and I see ePublishing as the media outlet of the future. While the benefits of eBooks and ePublishing are numerous (cost-efficiency, speed, forest preservation), I must admit that I am one of those old-fashioned people who feels nothing short of giddy when brushing open the feathery pages of a solid book."

Second Place

Yu Zheng
California, USA

Reality Hits

Like North Korea, China is not a free country. Those words stood out amid all the lines of text in the humanities textbook. My mind screamed denial, outrage, confusion. Reality had just hit me. Hard.

For almost as long as I could remember, I'd lived in the United States without forgetting my birth country, but I'd always been too young to realize the magnitude of the task, to balance my two cultures and live here without being an outsider but hang on to my home country's values. Before that day in sixth grade, I'd happily lived here while remaining truly Chinese, thinking it'd be no big deal.

That was until I'd found out what some people thought of a person who remained loyal to "not a free country." No, that article probably wasn't representative of people's attitudes, but it clearly labeled China as "not free," in a textbook that all my peers read. I'm sure the textbook was well-intentioned, but in any case it sets China in the same league with North Korea, and North Korea's own reputation is enough for many people to assume the same about China.

Despite living in the U.S. for the vast majority of my life, I never let go of my Chinese nationality or culture, and given the choice, I would choose remaining Chinese over any other citizenship. However, it wasn't until that day of reading that one article in the humanities textbook that I realized how much of an outsider I could potentially be.

I was a kid who declared, at that age, himself a

Chinese citizen for life. Nobody teased me at the time, but I could see the differences I had from all my other classmates, the most significant of which was that, although many of my peers were from China, I remained one of, if not the, only one who had spent so much time in the United States but never gave up Chinese culture and citizenship. One of my classmates was born in Beijing and came from two Chinese parents, and yet barely spoke Chinese, preferring to stay with the American lifestyle. I met one person who was born in Switzerland and yet only spoke English. My peers around me had families from every corner of the globe, but most of them were themselves American. No wonder I felt oddly alone.

To be truthful, being alone didn't affect me all that much; I had a tendency to stay by myself given the choice, and doing things by myself wasn't anything new. But then as my peers found out about my views, they began asking why. Most of these were polite "why?"s, and when I explained it was simply my choice, they backed off. But of course, not all of them were so polite, and I saw that one day when someone asked me "What's wrong with you?" when I showed my simple preference of 24-hour time, the standard of China, over the American standard 12-hour time. Later, I got weird looks when peers saw that my Internet accounts were in Chinese. Even if they didn't say anything, their body language showed clear bewilderment at my so-called "weird habits."

This came to a head in seventh grade, when a classmate started saying "I'm not f***ing Chinese." He insisted that it wasn't a racist comment when I confronted him, but there is no doubt about it when he then referred to China in front of me as "Your f***ing country."

About the same time, I started social networking for

the first time, and I began to notice racist comments on YouTube. I posted a comment on a soccer video; I don't remember my comment itself, but the reply I got was: "We don't give a f***. You f***ing Chinese are the cancer of the world." I realized that the Internet is where people take advantage of anonymity to spit out what they think of everything, the complete lack of facts only serving to show their blind following of stereotypes from the popular and undoubtedly uninformed opinion of China: communist, neglecting of human rights, slaves of Mao Zedong.

There are events such as the Tiananmen Square protests or the invasion of Tibet that give rise to these stereotypes, but they are then warped until the image of Chinese people is twisted beyond recognition. In fact, from my visits back, I see no evidence of excessive oppression or mindless ignorance. Granted, the Internet still routinely censors material, the government covers up embarrassing incidents, freedom of speech is still limited. I am not insisting that China is just as free as any other country, but I must say that it's not as bad as most people say, and I am insulted at the amount of prejudice that we "communist mainlanders" bear.

I am not, nor have I ever been contemptuous of the United States. My loyalty to China is simply a result of my personality's stubborn quality; what I start out with is what I usually stay with, but I can never convince people it's that way. In fact, I love both countries, and I would refuse equally vehemently to renounce the U.S.

It isn't easy, as I originally thought, to combine the values and culture of both countries. I have, for example, lamented for my entire life the fact that I cannot speak Chinese as well as I can English. I regret that I know far more about American culture than I do about Chinese. These are small things, but they wreak havoc on my conscience as I try to keep my choices balanced between the two and try not to neglect one. It has been a torrid journey trying to soul-search and figure out what I really think and what my own values are, and I don't believe that I've finished. What I can say is that nobody should look down on or underestimate the task of living in two contrasting cultures without neglecting one.

~~~~

Biography:
Yu, or Victor, as his friends call him, is a young student with high ambition; he aspires to be a famous writer or musician one day. In his free time, he watches soccer and plays piano. He is never afraid to do what he likes, even if it means bearing constant ridicule at his love for classical music. He has weird talents such as being double-jointed and being able to write in mirror writing.

Commentary on eBooks:
"I enjoy reading on the Amazon Kindle, and often I download sheet music off the Internet. I think that it's a practical idea and very convenient, as opposed to having to lug physical copies of heavy books."

Third Place

Courtney Ngai
California, USA

The Timelessness of Literature

"Still are thy pleasant voices, thy nightingales, awake;/ For Death, he taketh all away, but them he cannot take." The closing lines of Callimachus's "Elegy for Heraclitus" are an apt description of ancient Greek literature. *Antigone* by Sophocles, Ovid's "The Story of Daedalus and Icarus" and "The Story of Pyramus and Thisbe," along with four epigrams by various authors, are all tragic works in which death figures a prominent role. The authors lived and died centuries ago, but their "voices" are still awake in their writings.

Along with death, a woeful presentation of man's mortality is a theme that pervades all of these pieces. The epigrams contain lines such as "The life of man is like a summer's leaf," "Men have but a day of youth and life," and "Had I of life brief share? / Brief share had I too of its evil plight." The play *Antigone* and the two stories by Ovid share these elements as well. Anitgone's love for her brother causes her to disobey King Creon's order and leads to the suicides of Antigone, her fiancé (Creon's son), and Creon's wife. In one of Ovid's works, Icarus doesn't listen to his father's wise instructions and pays for it with his life. In the other piece by Ovid, Pyramus and Thisbe, lovers forbidden to marry by their parents, plan an elopement. Following a bizarre turn of events, Pyramus kills himself because he thinks Thisbe is dead, and Thisbe kills herself when she finds Pyramus dead.

The epigrams cause the reader to contemplate the

shortness and triviality of life. They also reflect the despondency the ancient Greeks felt concerning death, and even life. "Unhappy Dionysius" sums up the feeling with "Here lie I, Dionysius of Tarsus, / Who lived for sixty years and never married. / Would that my father hadn't." *Antigone* and Ovid's stories convey lessons about the consequences of disobedience and pride, and, depending on the reader's view, the devotion or the foolishness caused by love.

These pieces of literature, the earliest of which dates back to seven hundred years before Christ, have been read by generations since. How have the "voices" of the authors been able to survive the test of time? The lessons and stories are nothing new to the contemporary reader.

King Solomon of Israel reflected on the meaninglessness of life two centuries before the first of the epigrams was written. Most people are probably more acquainted with the story of Romeo and Juliet that parallels that of Pyramus and Thisbe than the actual one recounted by Ovid. But perhaps the very fact that the lessons and stories are nothing new is why they have been read and studied—people can still relate to them.

In the same way, modern literature of the last few hundred years—recent pieces compared with those from ancient Greece—will likely remain timeless. Not only do the authors write about things that people can relate to, but they, like the ancient Greek authors, give future generations a picture—if only a glimpse—of the era in which they lived. Though Death has taken or will take the creators of both ancient and modern masterpieces away, it cannot take away their voices.

Biography:
Courtney likes to read, climb, and play with her dog. She doesn't have a favorite subject in school, but likes English just because of the reading part.

Commentary on eBooks:
"I prefer to read printed books, but I do read books online if I don't have time to go to the library. I think they are all right, but I like the ease of flipping to a specific page I am looking for in a regular book."

Award of Excellence

Rachel Matheson
Ontario, Canada

The Finger of Blame Unjustly Pointed

Although tragic events are daily occurrences often originating from an undefined combination of fate and personal choice, they always revolve around certain individuals. These unpredictable twists in life often result in pointed fingers and responsibility undeservingly laid on those who were regrettably involved.

During the few days that Romeo and Juliet spent together, their lives were subject to petty feuds and grotesque murders. Since Friar Lawrence was witness to the events that led to the young lovers' tragic deaths, blame is often laid on him. Although the Friar played a significant role in these young lives, responsibility for their deaths cannot deservedly be given to him. Through an examination of Shakespeare's famous love story *Romeo and Juliet*, it will be seen that Friar Lawrence was not responsible for the tragic outcome of the play.

Responsibility for the disastrous end of Romeo and Juliet cannot be given to Friar Lawrence, because his actions were for the benefit of those around him. Throughout the play, Friar Lawrence made many decisions, all of which immediately helped those who requested it. His actions were carefully thought out and it is obvious that he never acted without consulting both his conscience and the will of God.

When asked to marry Romeo to Juliet, it can be observed that Friar Lawrence experienced an internal debate before conceding to join them in marriage, with his final decision made in the hope of creating peace between their families. Agreeing to their marriage, Friar Lawrence explained to Romeo, 'For this alliance may so happy prove,/To turn your households' rancour to pure love"(II, iii, 91-92). His final decision was made for the benefit of Verona, fulfilling his role as God-serving Friar and concerned civilian.

Furthermore, Friar Lawrence made a difficult decision when providing Juliet with the sleeping potion, saving her from immediate suicide and from any ethical wrongdoing that would come from marrying Paris when previously wedded. To save Juliet, Friar Lawrence said, "That cop'st with death himself to 'scape from it;/And if thou darest, I'll give thee remedy" (IV, ii, 75-75). Friar Lawrence made the only possible decision given the situation, and therefore cannot be held responsible for the final results. During the play, Friar Lawrence is simply fulfilling his duties to God and to Verona, so the responsibility for the catastrophic outcome of the play cannot be placed upon him.

Secondly, the devastating ending to Shakespeare's play was the unforeseeable consequence of choices made by other characters, and therefore the numerous deaths should not be allocated on Friar Lawrence. Since many characters in the play came to Friar Lawrence for help with their conflicts, his actions always reflected the demands of these individuals. Ceding to Romeo's intention to wed Juliet, Friar Lawrence observed, "For by your leaves, you should not stay alone" (II, vi, 36). The choice to be married was theirs, and Friar Lawrence only served in aiding to carry out their chosen task.

Also, after providing Juliet with a solution in the form of a sleeping potion, he immediately sent a letter informing Romeo of their risky plan. Due to an unlucky outbreak of the plague, the letter could not get through, so Friar Lawrence reacted to this fateful news in a way that would ideally help those involved. In despair, Friar Lawrence exclaimed to Friar John:

> *The letter was not nice, but full of charge*
> *Of dear important; and neglecting it*
> *May do much danger. (V, ii, 18-20)*

This sudden change in plan wasn't due to his mistakes, but he immediately altered his plan to produce the desired results. Throughout the play, Friar Lawrence was frequently acting as a result of fate or of choices made by other people, therefore blame for the tragedy cannot be placed upon him.

Finally, the first meeting of Romeo and Juliet can be identified as the triggering point for the tragic events that followed, therefore since he played no part in their first encounter, Friar Lawrence cannot be held responsible for the devastating outcome of the play. From the moment their eyes met, the relationship of these young lovers was evidently doomed, due to the rivalry between their families.

Had they been given the freedom to love as they pleased, it can be seen that the dreadful ending to their lives would not have come to pass, therefore their parents, Montague and Capulet, hold responsibility for the lovers' deaths. After learning that Romeo was a Montague, Juliet remarked, "My only love spring from my only hate" (I, v, 137-138). Had he not been a Montague, Juliet would have been free to love him, however their family's hatred created obstacles that eventually led to their doom.

After finding the dead bodies in the Capulet tomb, the Prince exclaimed, "Capulet, Montague,/ See what scourge is laid upon you hate" (V, iii, 290-291). As these two enemies heard the entire tale of their children's love, they finally acknowledged that it was their unjustified feud that wrought these deaths. Therefore, after a thorough analysis of the play, it can be seen that it is Montague and Capulet, rather than Friar Lawrence that should carry the blame for the outcome of this play.

After carefully examining the tragic play *Romeo and Juliet*, it can be seen that Friar Lawrence is not responsible for the outcome. As a man dedicated to God and to Verona, Friar Lawrence always acted for the benefit of others. His decisions were thought out and always deemed morally correct. Friar Lawrence was rarely the one to make the decision, but rather helped see choice through. Through careful research, it was seen that Montague and Capulet had a large influence over choices made, therefore carrying responsibility for the tragic ending. Many factors led to the awful ending of *Romeo and Juliet*, but after careful examination, the one thing that can be assured is that Friar Lawrence should not shoulder the blame for the calamitous ending of the play.

~~~~

Biography:
Rachel enjoys reading fiction and non-fiction, especially fantasy, and has a special place in her heart for historical fiction set during the reign of Henry VIII. She enjoys dancing, particularly ballet, and attends lessons each week. Rachel dreams of traveling the world and experiencing many different cultures. She can speak French, and is currently learning Spanish.

Commentary on eBooks:
"I lack knowledge on the subject of eBooks, however I find them intriguing. When I first heard about them, the concept of reading a book without actually flipping pages put me off, because that is part of the experience. I would be willing to try them, but have had no opportunity. I am curious to see how the experience differs from normal reading."

Honorable Mention

Julia LaFond
North Carolina, USA

The Spelling Bee

The home school spelling bee was about to begin. I shifted in my seat nervously. I knew that I had a good chance of winning, but the other spellers were good, and spelling bees involve copious amounts of chance.

I wasn't as nervous as Kayla, though. She told me that at her last spelling bee, she had misspelled her first word.

I looked around the room. There were four rows of chairs at the front of the room set aside for the spellers. I was sitting in the fourth row, in the second seat from my left. Nearly all the other seats were filled with home schoolers who, like me, were wearing numbers around their necks, indicating their order in the lineup of spellers. Two seats were empty, as two participants had gotten sick at the last minute.

I glanced at the small crowd of spectators, composed mostly of parents, and decided to focus on the three Judges' sitting at the folding table in front of the audience when it was my turn to spell a word. Since the spellers were supposed to look at the Judges' anyway, this wouldn't be difficult.

I was relieved when Mrs. Kertesz, after outlining the rules, announced that there would be a practice round. It would greatly reduce my chances of misspelling a word due to nervousness. Based on the expressions of the spellers around me, they had the same thought.

I shouldn't have worried. I spelled the practice word perfectly. In fact, I kept spelling my words correctly.

Somewhere in the middle of the bee, I got a scare.

"Umlaut," announced the pronouncer.

"Oonlout?" I said. I had never heard of that word, and I had no idea how to spell it.

"No, umlaut."

"Oh, umlaut." I had a vague memory of seeing it on the list of words that might be used on the word list. "Umlaut. U-M-L-A-U-T. Umlaut."

"That is correct."

I sighed, relieved, as I relinquished the microphone to the next speller.

On the other hand, I clearly remember receiving *allegro*. As it is a musical term, and I had been seeing it written out every day for about four years, I knew precisely how it was spelled. I rattled off the letters so quickly that it was a few seconds before the Judges' announced that I had spelled the word correctly.

Eventually, there were only five spellers. I was happy to see that Kayla, despite her fears, had spelled all her words correctly. Then she received the word *luau*.

I stifled a groan. I knew she wouldn't be able to spell it, and she misspelled the word. She added an extra *u*.

Suddenly, there was only one other speller. He had an odd way of hesitating after saying each word and letter, but apparently this hadn't kept him from spelling every word he received accurately. Then and there, we began a battle for the first-place trophy.

Finally, in the twenty-first round, he received the word *opossum*. I remember thinking that it was spelled *oppossum*. After hesitating, he said, "Opossum. O-P-O-S-S-O-M. Opossum."

"That is incorrect," Mrs. Kertesz said regretfully. "Opossum is spelled O-P-O-S-S-U-M." My heart dropped to about my shoes. I knew that if I had gotten *opossum,* I would have lost.

Then, addressing me, Mrs. Kertesz said, "This is the twenty-second round of the competition. If you spell the next word correctly, you will be the champion of the home school spelling bee."

The pronouncer said, "Cilantro."

My heart was beating quickly. I knew that I could spell this word. I even knew that cilantro was an herb I had planted several times. "Cilantro," I pronounced carefully. It wouldn't do to misspell it due to excitement. "C-I-L-A-N-T-R-O. Cilantro."

"That is correct. You are now the official champion of the home school spelling bee."

As Mrs. Kertesz went on to say what I, the first runner-up, and the second runner-up had won, I was beaming. I had won the spelling bee, and would be advancing to the regional level. But meanwhile, I would be having good food and chatting with people at the reception.

I still have the trophy. It's colored gold, and has a cartoonish bumble bee on it. I also have the number I wore, and the word list that the spellers received. But I most treasure the memory of my victory at the spelling bee after weeks of practice.

Biography:

Julia LaFond is homeschooled and entering the tenth grade. She has one older sister entering college, and a cat named Frances. Julia loves to read, but doesn't usually read recent literature. She is interested in science, and wants to be a scientist some day. She is currently taking Ninjutsu classes.

Commentary on eBooks:
"I don't know much about eBooks or ePublishing. Using the Internet does seem like a good way to make literature available to more readers. However, some consideration is required to circumvent problems such as the ease of copyright violations online and the adverse effects on institutes promoting the printed word."

Judges' Award

Victoria Newchurch
Texas, USA

Never Give Up

Life is not always an easy road to walk on. Sometimes a curve ball gets thrown your way and you strike out. You know the phrase from *A Cinderella Story*, "Don't let the fear of striking out keep you from playing the game"? Sometimes you may strike out in life but that does not give anyone the reason to give up and not play the game of life. We need to take risks and act as if today will be our last day on this earth. If we do not, we may be asking ourselves why we left ourselves out of that event or why we stayed home when we could have gone out to meet with friends. I learned this when I shunned everyone and decided not to play the game of life.

My family had just made a move from Ohio to Texas, just in time for my senior year in high school. I had to leave all of my best friends and the only high school I knew. I had to start all over again and was determined to make it work no matter how hard it would be. It was not until I actually got to Texas that I soon realized the current chapter I was living was one hundred times harder than I thought it would be to write. I started my senior year with no friends whatsoever and it was very depressing. I knew I had to make some, somehow. I joined Student Council and went to church more often, but nothing was happening and I still hadn't made any friends.

It was then I started to give up. I kept telling myself that I hated Texas and how I could not wait to get out of here for college. I was determined to live for the future and not the present. My plan was to go to school, work, church and sleep. I would keep to myself and not do any of the senior activities my school had to offer. I was not to have any friends, who needs them anyway? That was my attitude and I see now that it was a poor one. I was starting to throw away one of the most important and fun years of my life. It would be the last year of my freedom from bills and living on my own and I was choosing not to live it to the fullest.

I thought I would be happier by going through the motions of life and not actually living. Truly, it is not the right thing to do because later on in life I realized I would regret the decisions I made and how I did not at least try to enjoy my senior year of high school. In order for me look back later in life and be happy with the decisions I made, I really needed an attitude change and to turn how I was living completely around. Instead of not making the effort to make friends and not enjoy my senior year, I decided to do the complete opposite. I went to football games with a friend I made in one of my classes, I started taking ballet classes with another friend from class and I got even more involved with student council by participating in more of the activities they had to offer.

It just took a decision and a few changes to my daily routines and my life is so much more rewarding. Instead of being angry at the pitcher for striking me out with that curveball, I saw the changes in the pitch and adjusted my swing accordingly. This time I feel like I have hit a home run and could not be happier with how everything is turning out so far. I was living with the fear of striking out again for a moment and then I quickly realized that it is just not worth it to overlook the gifts of today and focus only what the future may bring. We do need to work and plan for the future. But yesterday is a canceled check, tomorrow is just a promissory note- we need to live for today, like it may be the last day of your life!

~~~~

Biography:
Victoria is a very strong girl. In the past five years she has had to deal with two cross country moves. When Hurricane Katrina hit, she and her family moved to Ohio. Two and a half years later, her father's job transferred the family to Texas. All throughout this process, she handled the situation very maturely. Because of those moves, she has become closer to her family members than she ever before!

Commentary on eBooks:
"Instead of having to carry around a huge book, why not just have an eBook? There are devices that are able to carry a various amount of books that are able to be carried all at once with ease. Having an eBook is environmentally smart because it uses no paper. It also saves space in your bag and it pays off in the long run. I recommend everyone to join the new craze of eBooks!"

PRESENTED BY:

http://www.epicorg.com

EPIC'S New Voices Young Writers
http://newvoicesyoungwriters.com/

**New Voices Young Writers Competition
opens for entries on August 1.**

Please check our website for more details